UNSTEREOTYPICALS

MORA (BOOK 1)

C. F. EDWARDS

D1522646

UNSTEREOTYPICAL PUBLISHING

I dedicate this book to my mother, Lena Edwards, she's the best mom ever. She believed in me before I believed in myself.

*"Life and death are in the power of **your** tongue.*

K. L. 9:99

1

DEAR DIARY

I hate my parents. They are the reason for all my pain. I know that sounds dramatic, but I blame them for my unattractive appearance and the frightening reflection that stares back at me in the mirror. Most children would be happy to go to a private school and live in a big beautiful home, but what good is that if you're unattractive and borderline crazy? Let's start with the unattractive part. Having material things is nice, but people treat you better and are kinder to you when you fit in with what they consider conventional beauty. When you look in the mirror and your reflection is hideous, unattractive, and unsightly, it can be damaging. Trust me; I know.

My name is Mora Manning, and I am grossly underweight. Yet my mother, Mary Anne, calls me lean. If the wind blew a little too hard, it would wrap me up in a tornado like Dorothy and I'd find myself in the middle of Oz trying to find my way home. My mediocre and impolite peers remind me of my ever so visible flaws by giving me nicknames. The boys call me "Dark and Buggly" referencing my big brown eyes and dark skin and the girls have coined the oh so creative and mentally stimulating, "Bora Mora," because my mother refuses to allow me to wear make-up, resulting in my plain and boring appearance. She says its toxins are harmful for my skin. I wear my thick, bristly hair in a big puffy ponytail at the top of my head with long bangs to distract from my oversized forehead. If I were a couple shades lighter, had contacts to replace my bifocal lenses, and received a relaxer that straighten my coarse bristly hair, maybe I might be attractive enough to find a boy who likes me.

I've begged my mother for two things for my seventeenth birthday. A relaxer, to straighten out this kinky hair and contacts. Apparently, it's unsanitary to stick pieces of plastic in your eye, and according to her my hair is thick and healthy. She's a beautician and specializes in healthy hair, but I don't care about thick and healthy hair. I want a relaxer, because it will straighten my coarse curls and not only make them more manageable—it will make me more beautiful. I often fantasize about having hair like the girls in those Pantene Pro-V commercials that dance in the wind.

Even a lace front wig would be an improvement to the hair I have. How else am I supposed to compete in this new school and new grade? These eleventh-grade girls look like supermodels. Long, straight, flowing hair rules the world.

Unfortunately, because of my mother's prehistoric beliefs, I have to continue to wear unattractive bifocal lenses and walk around with this big poof of healthy, but unmanaged hair on my head. I look like a dark-skinned Olive Oyl with glasses. The only difference is, I don't have a Popeye to save me from this pitiful existence. Mary Anne, my mother, has nice, wavy, flowing long hair like my sister Rain, so they don't understand what I'm going through. Now couple that with my unattractive name, and hopefully you understand why I'm unhappy. I mean, who names their child Mora? It sounds like a rip off Dora doll that you buy at one of those second-hand stores. Why couldn't I be a Marissa or an Emily? They named my sister Rain Falls, while I'm Mora Lyndora. Apparently, I'm named after some great-great grandparent that I have never had the pleasure of meeting.

Now let's discuss the crazy part. Did I tell you I see ghosts and experience vivid nightmares that cause me to wake-up drenched in sweat and on the verge of a panic attack? I also received strange, cryptic text that seem to deliver the same message: "Be quiet."

They disappear when I show them to others and reappear when I view them alone.

My earliest memory of seeing a ghost was at eight. One night while I slept, the abrupt slamming of my bedroom door awakened me. My parents allowed me to keep my door open so the light from the hallway would spill over into my bedroom. They thought a little light might ease my imagination and keep me from hijacking their bed and inundating them with my late-night screams. When the door slammed shut, I jumped up, backed up against my headboard, and pulled my knees as close to my chest as possible. My quivering fingers held my plush blankets just high enough to cover my face but low enough to keep my eyes visible. As my eyes peered through the darkness, I caught a glimpse of moonlight. It crept through the open curtains, like a thief tiptoeing in the night. I thought the draft from the enormous bay window in the corner of my room might have been the culprit, but when I looked at my window, it was closed—and right before me was a ghost hovering above the floor. I nearly screamed, but when I opened my mouth, no sound came forth. The ghost had coarse thick hair that was put into a ponytail and big round eyes covered by spectacles. It floated toward me and was wearing a long night gown identical to mine. The gown danced around her without the aid of wind. I can still envision her solemn face. It resembled mine but was void of color. She didn't smile, and she moved as if she was in slow motion. It looked like me, if I were reimagined in one of those black and white movies from the '40s and '50s that my mother loved to watch. She had my rounded nose, hair style and my facial expression. It was terrifying. She raised one of her folded hands in front of her, brought it to her mouth, and pressed her long and wrinkled index finger against her crusted black lips. I can still smell the odor that her presence produced. It was like black tar being repaved on an old road.

On many of those nights when I had nightmares and received those unfamiliar text notifications, I would scream and run into my parents' room, but this time I froze. My fear cemented my legs to the ground. She crept toward me; her index finger still pressed against her lips. The closer she approached, the more fearful I became. When she was halfway toward my bed, she stopped and placed her hand down in front of her. My racing heartbeat slowed, and for a moment I thought she would leave and go about her business. Then, she dashed toward me and pressed her face toward mine and said, "Shh..., Mora!!" in a petrifying and spine-chilling tone that sounded like a child's voice. I screamed so loud that my mother and father ran into my room and tried to calm me down, but she dissipated into the air like an early morning mist. At first, my parents responded as any parent would. They consoled me and told me it was just a nightmare and that if I stopped reading horror novels and watching scary movies, it would go away. So, I followed their suggestions and traded my horror novels for romance. But the ghost sightings and nightmares didn't stop. They kept happening. My parents made me believe that something was wrong with me, and I believed it too. They made me question if my idiosyncratic behavior was responsible for the dissolution of their marriage.

Then one day not long after the incident, my parents called me down from my room and told me they were taking me to see a psychiatrist. Since my father was a psychiatrist, **The American Medical Association** considered it unethical for him to treat me, so he referred me to one of his colleagues. I had to decide. Would I lie or tell the truth? I broke down in my best fake cry and told them I was doing it for attention. I quoted an article from **Psychology Weekly** that talked about child abandonment issues and being an insecure attachment. Yes. I lied, but I would not be ugly and crazy. Ugly mocha girls that are crazy end up in mental asylums or small cramped jail cells. Pretty girls that are crazy become pop stars who get a slap on the wrist and go to rehab. So, I did *what any scared child would do: I stopped telling my parents about my weird occurrences, but that didn't stop the occurrences from continuing, and it didn't stop them from taking me to see a psychiatrist. A few days later, I was on medication. At first, all the abnormal occurrences stopped, but it wasn't long before it all started happening again. The nightmares, ghost and text messages became more frequent and got stronger and more intimidating with each encounter. I knew I was unattractive, but now I wondered if I was losing my mind.*

2

SIGNS

*M*ora closed her big brown eyes, took a deep breath, and boarded the crowded and noisy school bus. As she watched her high school peers adorned in ghost, demon, and devil costumes in preparation of Halloween, fear enclosed in around her. Although her body was physically on the bus, an unforgettable memory from last night's dream invaded her mind. The abrupt rain that beat against the bus's windows was another potent trigger that reminded her of the rain that beat aggressively against her window in her dream. She struggled to stay focused on the present as her reoccurring nightmare infested her thoughts. It dragged her from conscious into unconscious. Within seconds, Mora was in a trancelike state, reliving the vivid nightmare from the last few nights.

She dreamed that a familiar ghost-like entity who resembled her was in her room, but this time its demeanor was not solemn and serene. She felt its malice as she could feel someone's negative vibe when in a dreadful mood. On previous occasions, Mora knew it was a ghost by the way it moved, but this time it was not floating in the air. It looked like it was standing and had a more statuesque form. Its back was turned away from her. The evil that discharged from its body suffocated her. Mora likened its presence to a multitude of dark human energies, absent their bodies. Her neck tightened as adrenaline rushed through her body. She breathed faster and harder. The rhythm of her heartbeat escalated to levels she had never experienced. She placed her hand over her chest and took long slow breaths to calm herself, but she was still frightened. The entity wore a long, flowing black nightgown that hung all the way to the floor. The apparition's hair was identical to Mora's. It was in a big, puffy, and bristly ponytail at the crown of her head. A loud continuous clicking sound echoed through the room. It mimicked the ticking sound a stove made before a fire ignited on one of its burners. The movement of the ghost-like entity was in sync with the bizarre sound. With every movement it made, a click followed. Mora knew that whenever she heard the sound, the entity was moving toward her. When the ghost-like entity turned its head toward Mora, its neck made a *click... click...click... clicking* sound. It looked like her evil twin. It had bangs that covered its forehead just like Mora, and a few loose tendrils of hair hung along the sides of her face. Its eyes were black, round, and hollow and its teeth were Tic Tac white, which was a sharp contrast to its mocha and porcelain like skin. It resembled a real-life evil doll. Its movements were sporadic and stutter like. Its face was only visible because of the streetlight that shone through Mora's window. It stood in the corner by the unopened window, yet somehow a sharp chill swept through the room which caused the spirit's gown to rise and fall as if it was doing so independently and of its own volition. She lifted her small wrinkled right hand and placed her index finger against her crusted black lips. The sound it made was like sandpaper rubbing against wood. She stroked her finger in an up and down motion against her lips and black dust particles fell from them like sawdust to the floor. Mora stared at the ghost-like entity with a apprehensive expression, unsure of the message she was seeking to communicate. At first, the demented ghost-like figure stood in the back corner of her room between her big bay window and her mahogany dresser. But every night in her dream, it would move a few feet closer.

With every step, its presence grew stronger, and the clicking sound became louder and more pronounced with every movement. Mora closed her eyes, covered her ears, and wished that it would go away.

Mora turned her head to her bedroom door and wondered if she could outrun it. She pulled the covers off of her body and slid her left leg out of the bed, while keeping a close watch on the entity. It was moving closer, but ever so slowly. As she put her first feet on the floor, the apparition took its index finger from off its lips and moved her finger from left to right like a mother would to her naughty daughter. Mora ignored the warning and dashed for the door. As she ran, a tingling sensation crept down from her knee until it reached her feet. It was as if her legs had fallen asleep. She fell to her knees and her left cheek collided hard against the hardwood floor. A single tear escaped her eye, and the cold rough breaths from the apparition like entity blew on the back of her neck. Every time Mora stood up, she fell to the ground, her legs still asleep. As she reached for the doorknob, she felt a strong tug on her night gown. She opened her mouth to scream, but just as she did a frigid hand wrapped itself around the base of her throat. Its fingers lengthened and circled around her neck until it reached her mouth and muted her sound. The entity picked up Mora and threw her down on her bed. Mora closed her eyes, afraid of its appearance. She tried to scream, but the harder she tried, the more forceful the phantom's hands pushed against her face. The artic chill of its breath against her face gave her shivers. It floated above her bed, its body directly parallel with Mora's. The apparition-like entity kept one hand wrapped tightly against Mora's throat and used the other to signal her to be silent. Its hand pushing firmly against her throat. She prayed that it would release her and hoped that the oily residue would not continue to drip on her skin. Every drop felt like freezing water. The scent she emitted was no longer of black tar; it now smelled of decayed flesh. It was so foul she thought she would vomit. The apparition released a loud sound. "Shh!!," it uttered. The sound was so disturbing, it caused Mora to open her eyes. Mora's fear paralyzed her. She attempted to move, but no matter how hard she tried, she could not move her body. The apparition's grip tightened against her throat. She tried to move her feet, then her legs. She had no control. It was like a waking version of sleep paralysis. The worst she had ever experienced. Out of the corner of her eye, she saw shadows of someone's footsteps from underneath the crack of the door. The ghost-like figure slowly turned its head toward the door. *Click, click, click, click,* was the sound her neck made. The doorknob moved, and the ghost like entity released its grip on Mora and disappeared. Mora's voice returned and she let out an uncontrollable and piercing scream. When Mora returned to consciousness, she was standing on the bus, and over one-hundred eyes were staring at her. *Did I just scream like a lunatic on the bus?*

Mora scanned the bus in search of a single seat. She preferred sitting alone. She noticed an empty one in the back. She held her head low to avoid eye contact, threw the hood of her purple pea coat over her head and hurried toward the empty seat. Curious eyes watched her as she made her way down the aisle of the congested school bus. Normally, she preferred her own scent and despised the stench of musty boys who smelled of wet dogs and cheerleaders who wore too much perfume, but it was a pleasant distraction from the dreadful smell from her nightmares. It had been years since she had taken a bus, and now she knew why. The silent judgement coupled with concentrated glances from her peers made her uncomfortable. *If my father had arrived on time, I wouldn't be in this predicament!* She contemplated walking home but knew that her hair and make-up would not survive the onslaught of rain that speedily fell on the roof of the school bus. She gripped her backpack with both hands, held her breath, and continued down the bus aisle. One student threw his backpack in the empty seat next to him, which resulted in laughter from a few of the surrounding students.

"Find another seat Dark and Buggly," he replied. Mora stopped and glanced at him as he turned his attention to the game he was playing on his phone. She thought about grabbing his phone and throwing it out of the bus window, then imagined grabbing his golden ponytail, wrapping it around her small mocha fingers, and pulling it so hard that he fell out of his seat. Instead, she focused on the words of her psychiatrist: "Feel the anger; but don't act on it." Mora took a deep breath, let the anger pass, and continued toward her intended destination.

The double seat all the way in the back was empty, she hurried to grab it before someone else would. Once she reached her desired seat, she plopped down on the hard-cushioned seat, placed her backpack on the floor in front of her, and peered down the aisle to see if her peers were watching. They were not. They had their heads glued to their mobile devices and tablets. Mora sighed in relief and reached into her backpack for her ear buds. She smiled when her fingers touched the square case that contained them. These two little devices were her sanctuary. They provided her refuge in a time of trouble. She placed her earbuds in her ear and listened to her favorite classic solemn R&B jam, "I Tried", by Brandy. Its smooth baseline and intricate strings provided just the right amount of tranquility she needed. She closed her eyes and listened as the drumming of the raindrops moved in sync with the bass of the song. Her wish had come true. She had her own seat and was uninterrupted. Mora placed her head against the window and put her feet on the empty cushion beside her, cautious not to mess up her hair or smear her makeup. Her cell phone buzzed in her pocket, and she froze. She had a sound inkling of who it was because she always got a notification on her cell after a nightmare or ghost sighting. Mora ignored it, but it kept vibrating. She powered it off and put it back in her pocket. *It's just a coincidence,* she thought.

Mora was overjoyed when the bus driver closed his door and the bus moved. It relieved her because the longer he stayed, the greater probability she would have to share her seat. Mora contemplated checking the text message just in case it was her father calling to say he was in the parking lot, but had a powerful feeling in the pit of her stomach that it was another warning telling her to, "Be quiet." She ignored it and put her attention on her music. She raised the volume of her music to its peak. Its loudness kept her mind focused on the present. She noticed that when she gave her attention to things she enjoyed, the dreams appeared to be less powerful and the thoughts surrounding them less frequent. One of her classmates nudged his friend, stood up and pointed to a girl running alongside of the bus. She was hitting the door with her fist and yelling at the top of her lungs.

"Wait! Wait!" she yelled. Mora looked out of her window. She saw a large beefy frame holding an umbrella trying to catch the bus. *Please don't open the door. I really don't want to share my seat today,* Mora thought to herself. The bus driver stopped the bus and opened his doors. Candice made her way on to the already crowded bus, huffing and heaving as if she were about to cough up a lung. Mora sunk down in her seat and hoped that she had not seen her. *When did she return to school?*

Candice was a burly girl with a smooth cinnamon skin tone. She wore her hair in long corn-rows down the middle of her back and had on the same nylon sweats she often wore. They made an awkward swishing sound that always pre-announced her arrival. Her shoelaces were untied, and her shoes leaned over when she walked. The best word to describe her was, 'unkempt.' She looked like a grown woman in kid's clothes. She was a husky, meaty girl.

Although Mora did not envy Candice, she always wondered how she gained so much weight because despite her own voracious appetite she remained thin and boney. Candice smacked her gum loudly and always appeared to have enough gum for three people within those fat cheeks. She desperately needed a dentist, and everyone knew it because every time she opened her mouth, she unknowingly revealed a plethora of cavities. She was the school bully, and everyone followed her commands, or they would face the wrath of her fist, righty and lefty. As she walked down the aisle, people moved their backpacks to offer her a seat. Normally, she would randomly push people or smack freshmen upside the head, but something was different about her today. She had a smile on her face. As she walked past everyone, she smiled and nodded her head. It made everyone nervous. Her frown was typically a scowl, and she uttered unkind words. This fresh behavior change was strange and sparked curiosity among the students. They whispered and talked amongst themselves as they turned their undivided attention toward her. Candice arrived at the back seat where Mora sat and waited for her to speak. She looked down at Mora with her feet in both seats and her head against the window. She pondered her words before speaking. Billy moved his blond locks from his face and turned around in his seat to get a better look at Candice.

"This is about to get interesting," he whispered to the girl sitting next to him.

"More than interesting," she replied. Candice twiddled with her thumbs and nervously bit her bottom lip before speaking.

"Is this seat taken?" Candice asked, politely. Mora had her eyes closed and her face turned toward the window. She tried her best to ignore Candice and let her music occupy all her attention. She slowly bobbed her head to the beat. Candice moved a step further. She lightly tapped Mora's shoe, and immediately Mora's eyes opened. *Here we go.* Mora moved her feet, and took her scarf from around her neck, and wiped the droplets of water and any debris from off the seat and scooted as far to the window as possible. There was a prolonged silence between the two girls. Mora looked straight ahead. All the students on the bus stared at them as if they were spectators at a boxing match waiting for their favorite fighter to take their first hit. Mora subtly took out her ear buds, clasped them in her palm, and held them in front of her.

"Nice ear buds," stated Candice. Mora rolled her eyes and sighed heavily. She opened up her hand and threw the ear buds on the seat next to Candice.

Mora folded her arms and leaned her head back against the window.

"You were just going to take them anyway," Mora whispered.

Candice kindly handed the earbuds back to Mora. "I want to apologize for how I treated you." Mora lifted her head off of the bus window and turned toward Candice. She pushed her glasses a little further down her button nose to get a clearer view of her facial expression. She was unfamiliar with Candice's kinder, more human-like tone.

"Excuse me?" Mora replied. Candice took a deep breath and started again.

"I'm sorry for picking on you; it was wrong. Could you find it in your heart to forgive me?" she asked. She stared at the floor to hide the tears that welled in her eyes.

"Is this a joke?" Mora asked. Candice wiped her eyes and scooted close to Mora. She wanted to have a private conversation. She turned, expecting someone to be behind her.

"It's not a joke. Something horrible happened to me when I was away and made me realize the error of my ways." Candice grasped Mora by the arm and wrapped her large fingers around Mora's fragile wrist. "You need to forgive me, Mora; for your own good," Mora pulled her arm to get out of Candice's grasp, but she was too strong for her.

"Let me go; you're hurting me," Mora replied. Candice quickly released Mora when she realized that she had grabbed her too strongly.

"I'm sorry; I didn't mean to hurt you." Mora snatched her backpack from off the ground and stood up.

"You meant to hurt me because you're a bully. I'm tired of you putting your hands on me and stealing my things!" Mora yelled.

"I really didn't mean it this time; I'm trying to protect you," Candice replied.

"Protect me? The only person I need protection from is you. Now move over and let me out," Mora demanded. More students on the bus turned around in their seats to watch the heated argument between Mora and Candice. Most of them had heard rumors about brave students standing up to Candice, but had never seen someone talk back, let alone yell at Candice in person. Candice inched closer toward Mora before uttering her next words.

"If you don't forgive me, dreadful things will happen to you," Candice whispered softly.

"What are you going to do, eat me?" Mora taunted. The once quiet bus burst into extreme laughter. Candice's smile faded. Her cinnamon cheeks were now a scarlet red. She squinted her eyes, clenched her fist, and bit her bottom lip. The last person who had spoken to Candice in that tone, Jimmy Dalton, was beat up so badly he was hospitalized. Candice closed her eyes and breathed slow breaths. They watched as her enormous chest rose and fell with each inhale and exhale. The students' eyes widened as they whispered amongst themselves. They speculated on how Candice would beat Mora this time. Then something unexpected happened. Candice unclenched her fist and in a soft tone she repeated the mantra, "I love everyone, and everyone loves me."

Candice continued her positive affirmations until her mood shifted. She opened her eyes and stared at Mora for a few seconds and pondered how she would proceed. Mora's behavior conflicted her. On one hand, she did not want Mora to win the argument and risk being humiliated in front of her peers. But she knew that if she acted as she previously had, there would be consequences ... dire ones. Candice moved out of the way and let her leave. Mora put her earbuds in her pocket and walked away. The students were astonished that Candice let Mora talk back, and disappointed there would be no physical exchange of fist.

Mora was pleased that she had stood up for

herself. She walked down the bus aisle with her head held high and her back straight. When she reached the front of the bus. She tapped the bus driver on the shoulder.

"Could you open the door?" Mora asked.

"Are you sure you want to walk in this weather?" the bus driver replied.

"It beats sitting on the bus with her and I'm only a couple hundred feet from the school," Mora replied.

"Suit yourself," the bus driver replied. He opened the door. Mora turned toward the back of the bus and gave Candice the middle finger.

Billy turned toward the girl next to him and whispered, "Little Mora just punked Big Candice," As soon as Candice heard the response. Her breathing became heavy, and her face turned from a light cinnamon to a scarlet red. She jumped up from her seat and charged toward the front of the bus at full speed toward Mora, but as. soon as she reached the middle of the bus, she slipped on her shoestring and fell hard on her back. The students on the bus burst into roaring laughter while Mora ran off the bus and onto the wet pavement. The thought of Candice falling on the bus made her smile, "That's what her fat butt gets," Mora whispered to herself.

3

VOICES

*I*t seemed that as soon as Mora stepped off the bus, the rain fell at a more rapid pace. Mora removed her umbrella from her backpack and opened it as soon as she stepped out into the inclement weather. She tilted her purple umbrella at a ninety-degree angle so it would block her face and shield her hair from the cold wet droplets that could collide against her skin. Mora dodged puddles and avoided falling as she slipped on oily and wet patches of pavement. Light rain was in the forecast, but she had not expected the vigorous wind and harsh rainfall. As Mora climbed the steps to her school, Andorra Christian Academy, a forceful gust of wind hurled her umbrella out of her hand. It skipped across the parking lot. Mora ran after it, but every time she got close enough to grab it, it moved a few feet from her. By the time she caught it, her hair was wet, and her foundation was running down her face.

A frustrated Mora rushed toward the school door, pushed it open, and ran straight toward the girl's bathroom. She used her umbrella to shield her face from any of her potential peers. The water from her soaked white blouse and checkered purple and grey skirt dripped all over the freshly waxed school floors. Her water-laden loafers left puddles of water and remnants of mud tracks on the floor. Just as Mora was about to enter the bathroom, three eleventh grade girls by the name of Sarah, Emily and Marissa came from out of the bathroom. Their skin tones mimicked the hues of peach, vanilla, and caramel. They exited the bathroom wearing matching cheerleading costumes. They appeared to be dressed as triplets although they looked nothing alike. They pushed their long, beautiful locks of hair behind their ears as if they had spent hours rehearsing the simplistic and overdone motion. Mora watched as the three girls scurried away from her as if she were plagued with some uncurable, contagious disease. She admired their busty chest, long straight hair, and light skin tones, but resented the freedom they had to experiment with their looks. As she entered the bathroom, she heard the girls snicker and whisper behind her back. She stayed out of view, but close enough to the door to hear what they said.

"Oh my, is that the new girl Mora everyone was talking about? She's hideous," replied Sarah.

"Quit overreacting Sarah, she's not hideous. She's just not cute. She has more of a boring look," Marissa replied.

"So, you're saying she's a Bora Mora?" Sarah asked. All the girls broke out into incessant giggles.

"Well, apparently her father's like some world renown psychiatrist and is loaded. He's like the best in the world," Emily replied.

"Then why doesn't she use some of that wealth to change her look?" asked Sarah.

"Who knows, but if my father had as much money as hers, I wouldn't be walking around looking like a dark-skinned Olive Oyl. She'd be half-way decent looking with a relaxer, a new nose, and a push up bra," commented Marissa.

"The one's with money never know what to do with it," Emily replied.

"Isn't that the truth?" agreed Sarah. The girls looked each other over. They hiked up their miniskirts a little higher, added lip stick to their collagen injected lips, and continued down the hall with their schoolbooks in their hand.

When Mora no longer heard them speaking, she

dropped her backpack and umbrella on the ground, and went straight to the bathroom mirror. She fought back her urge to cry as she dried the specs of rain drops from her glasses with a piece of tissue from her peacoat pocket. She grabbed paper towels from the dispenser and removed some of the make-up that dribbled onto her blouse. Mora glanced at her disheveled reflection and banged her fist on the bathroom sink. Irritated, she opened her mouth and let out a bellowing yell that echoed throughout the bathroom. She yanked her backpack off the ground, took out her half comb, half brush and her small make-up compact and violently combed her hair. Splashes of water splattered on the mirror with each stroke.

"I hate my damn hair, and I hate the rain!" she yelled. Mora took a section of her hair and ran the combed through it repeatedly. The harder she combed, the more pain she felt. It had returned to its tight curls, and the only way to revert to its original style was to straighten it again. "This is my father's fault, if he was on time, I wouldn't have had to walk in the rain, deal with Candice and hear mean words from the most popular girls in school," she mumbled. Mora slammed the brush against the counter and stared at herself in the mirror. She pointed her finger at her reflection. "And if you didn't have dark blotchy skin and coarse hair, I wouldn't have to straighten my hair, lighten my skin and wear make-up. I could be beautiful." She snatched the brush from off the counter and struck the mirror with it. It cracked, and a medium-sized piece of glass near the bottom of the mirror fell and cut the palm of her hand before it shattered in the sink. Untamed wailings escaped her throat as she held her injured hand and the tears, she tried to hold from earlier flowed from her eyes.

Drops of her precious, red blood dripped into the sink. She grabbed a few paper towels and applied pressure to soak up the blood. After a few gentle presses, the bleeding stopped. She picked up the remaining pieces of glass, wrapped them in paper towels, and threw them in the trash. When she returned to the sink, she turned on the water, and splashed warm water over the blood droplets. Once the sink was clean, she noticed a couple drops of blood on the floor. In a hurry to leave the bathroom, she bent over and wiped up the remaining blood. A raspy, child-like, unfamiliar and whispering voice pierced through the serene silence of the bathroom. "Why do you speak unkind words to me, Mora?" the voice asked. Its echo ricocheted off the bathroom walls. Mora stood up and turned her head toward the bathroom door. She expected some student or school administrator to be standing in the doorway, but no one was there. Mora pushed her glasses up close to her face and did a 360-degree turn around the bathroom.

"Who's calling my name?" she stuttered. There was no response. Mora's heartbeat increased. Her lips quivered and her breaths were sharp and swift. To calm herself, she closed her eyes and took a deep breath and placed her hand on her heart to monitor its rhythm. She crept toward the bathroom stalls and wondered who would orchestrate such a frightening scare on Halloween. One by one, she pushed open the stall doors. Icy shivers traveled down her arms as she heard the door creak. Once it was fully open, she looked inside, and no one was there. Unable to take any more suspense, she opened the remaining two doors, but they were also empty. She nervously swallowed a huge gulp of air which resulted in a dry cough. The temperature in the bathroom dropped, which resulted in raised goosebumps on her arms. Mora picked up her backpack, and jetted for the door. The light bulbs in the bathroom burst, and shards of glass fell like confetti from the ceiling. Mora tripped over her umbrella and fell to the ground and covered her head to shield herself from the raining glass.

"Sticks and stones rarely break bones, but your unkind words will make me harm you," the raspy unidentified voice chanted. Once she heard the last glass piece fall, she hopped up off the floor. As she gazed directly in front of the cracked mirror, a sharp chill shot through her body. Her reflection was no longer staring back at her: it had been replaced by the apparition like entity from her dream. Its eyes were no longer black, they were scarlet red. She had long crystal yellow nails, and her bangs fell just above her eyelids. Mora opened her mouth to scream, but no sound came forth. Her feet felt like they were cemented to the floor and wouldn't budge, no matter how hard she tried to move. The reflection-girl stood there with the same bristly hair, purple spectacles, and dirty blouse that Mora was wearing. Next, Mora heard the click... click... clicking sound as it slowly and rigidly lifted both its hands from its side. It reached out its arms toward Mora and walked closer toward her. Mora wiggled her legs and they moved. She ran at lightning speed and snatched up her backpack from the floor that was in the door's pathway. She jetted down the lengthy dark hallway. Ear-piercing screams exploded from her lungs and echoed throughout the school. Her nightmares had manifested, and her fear was suffocating her. She could barely breathe, but she kept running. Strong footsteps chased behind her. At first the steps sounded like a fast-paced walk, it then morphed into a light jog, and then transformed to a full-on sprint. Mora picked up her pace.

"Come back! Come back!" an unfamiliar voice yelled.

Mora did not turn around. Something within her broke, and she received her second wind. She threw her backpack on the ground and was now running like a track star. Her hands were like fan blades as they moved back and forth alongside her slim frame. Mora heard the footsteps draw nearer. Her heart was about to explode through her chest. The sound of her loafers clicked rapidly against the hard surface of the school floor. When the school front door was in view, a sense of relief washed over her. Her relief changed to chills when a strong, cold, and wet hand gripped its long fingers on her shoulder.

4

THE FIGHT

*M*ora closed her eyes, balled her fists and turned around swinging both her arms in a circular motion. The force of her fist collided with solid flesh and hard bone. She only stopped swinging when she heard noises that sounded like human wailings. Unsure of what to expect, she opened her eyes one at a time. Mora was embarrassed. There laid a boy on the floor in a fetal position. His dark coffee-colored hands covered his head to block himself from the onslaught of Mora's consistent and rapid blows. He gasped for air. When the young man didn't feel anymore fist punching his skin, he removed his arms from over his head. Mora admired his smooth skin and his abundant, dark, curly locks. She leaned forward and placed one hand on her knee and the other on her

39

heart. As her breathing slowed, she straightened up and cut the unknown boy a frosty glance.

"What's wrong with you? You don't chase after girls in dark buildings, especially on Halloween," scolded Mora.

"I wanted to return this. Besides, it's not dark in this building," he countered. Mora looked up and the light bulbs were now bright and beaming. She was confused. The young man held out his arm toward Mora. Grasped between his fingers was a leather-bound notebook embroidered with purple and gold writing. Mora snatched it from his hand. She turned the journal over and checked the lock on her diary. The youthful man dusted off his jeans and picked himself off of the ground.

"I wouldn't read your journal, because I definitely wouldn't want anyone to read mine." *He keeps a journal?* She wanted to be angry, but as she gazed into his grey eyes and admired his thick dark eyebrows and his barely there mustache, her anger melted like a bag of ice being kissed by the rays of the sun. The pubescent boy took his left hand and pushed his curly locks out of his face. His cartoonish dimples became even more pronounced when he flashed Mora a smile. "My name is Edward," he replied. He extended his hand toward Mora. Mora hesitated. She had not forgiven him for frightening her, but she did not want to appear rude. She accepted his hand. His grip was soft, yet firm.

"I'm Mora," she replied. She slipped her hand out of his as if holding it was some forbidden sin.

"I know your name," he replied.

"Excuse me?" Mora questioned.

"You always score higher than me on every test in Mrs. Dudley's Latin class. You probably don't recognize me because I sit in the back and normally have on the green baseball cap," Edward said. Mora placed her hand on her chin and imagined all the people in her class and smiled when she got a hint of who she thought he might be.

"Do you wear glasses?" Mora questioned.

"Yeah, but I got contacts recently," Edward replied.

"You look different," Mora responded.

"Is that good?" Edward asked curiously.

"Not good or bad, just different," Mora replied.

"Oh, well your journal fell from your backpack and I just wanted to return it," Edward responded with disappointment in his tone. Mora looked down the hallway; her belongings were scattered across the floor. She kneeled down and picked up her favorite purple pen. Edward followed her lead and helped her gather the remainder of the contents that had fallen from her backpack. Her bathroom encounter

C. F. EDWARDS

was still etched in her mind. Mora wanted to tell him what she witnessed in the bathroom because she did not want to harbor her fear alone. She decided to keep her secret to herself, because divulging something so weird and personal could give him the wrong impression.

"Why were you running so fast? Where you trying to catch the bus or something?"

"I didn't want to miss my ride. It's no fun walking home in the rain." Mora and Edward both reached for the last piece of paper, when he noticed a few trickles of blood on her hand.

"What happened?" he asked. Mora combed through her mind for a believable answer. She did not want to reveal anything about her bathroom encounter or that she had damaged school property.

"I cut myself on my compact mirror," she stuttered.

"Let me grab my first aid kit in my backpack. I'll be right back."

"What kind of kid carries a first aid-kit to school?"

"A kid with an overprotective mother."

"Tell me about it," Mora mumbled. They both locked eyes and smiled. Mora turned her head away and broke from his glance.

"It's okay. I have some tissue in my pocket," Mora

42

replied. Mora reached for her pocket, but Edward intercepted her hand. His soft skin against hers, gave her goosebumps-the welcomed kind.

"You don't want to get blood on that beautiful pea coat," Edward replied. Edward then reached into her right pocket and felt around until his fingers touched something soft. He removed the tissue from her pocket and held it above her hand.

"May I?" he asked.

Mora nodded and gave him the okay. She gazed into Edward's grey chestnut-shaped eyes. He placed his hand on top of hers and lightly dabbed her wound until the blood was no longer dripping. Edward looked up at her and smiled. His sculpted dimples complimented his perfectly chiseled cheek bones. Mora had a tingling sensation in her stomach. It was similar to the feeling Rebecca from her *Butterflyz* novel felt when she laid eyes on Chance for the first time at the Winter Ball. Edward's skin felt like a new silk blouse being worn for the first time as it glided across Mora's skin. She broke her gaze frequently to make sure she was not staring at him.

"Why do you keep smiling at me? It makes me uncomfortable," Mora responded.

"I think you're cute." Mora removed her hand from his and rolled her eyes.

"Now you're just mocking me," she replied.

"Did I say something wrong?" Edward asked, confused.

"How could anyone who looks like me be cute?" Mora questioned.

"What do you mean look like you?" Edward asked.

"You know, dark-skinned with this hair and runny make-up. Not to mention these horrendous glasses," she added.

"Everybody has unpleasant hair days; do you see this mountain of girl hair I have. The guys tease me about it every day. The only reason I don't have my hat on is because I left it at home, I can't wait till my parents let me cut it. By the way, I like mocha. They name beverages after your skin tone," Edward replied.

"Don't cut it; your hair is perfect," Mora blurted out.

"You think my hair is perfect?" Edward questioned.

"I think you got the wrong impression, you're not my type," Mora jabbed. Edward took a few steps back from Mora. A prolonged silence lingered between them. His smile faded, shoulders dropped, and he no longer made eye contact. He put his hands in his pocket and shifted his weight from one foot to the next.

"It was nice meeting you, but I'm going to head back to chess club," replied Edward. He handed her the rest of her things and turned around and headed in the other direction. Mora let out a lengthy sigh and watched him drop his head and nonchalantly saunter down the hall. Her guilt ate at her for being cruel to someone who had shown her nothing but kindness. Mora cupped her hands over her mouth and yelled.

"Maybe we can study Latin sometime," Edward stopped turned around and lifted his head up. His smile returned.

"I'd like that," he replied. Edward walked toward Mora. He pushed his black curls from out of his face.

"I'm having a Halloween party this evening. It's just a few friends and no one's dressing up. You want to stop by?" Edward asked.

"I'd love to," Mora replied. Edward took out his phone, unlocked the code, and handed it to Mora. Mora typed her number in the phone and saved it under her name and handed it back to him.

"I just texted you," replied Edward. Mora took her phone from her coat pocket and read the text from Edward but also saw a text from an unidentified number that read "998". She stared at her phone with a puzzled expression.

"Is everything okay?" Edward asked.

"Yeah, just a text from a wrong number," Mora replied.

"I'll call you in a couple hours to give you the address; I'm must get back to the chess club meeting," Edward responded.

"Postea te videbo," Mora replied.

"Looking forward to seeing you later too," Edward walked backwards and watched Mora until she walked out of the building. Once she left, he headed in the opposite direction with a huge smile on his face.

5

THE WALK

*I*f there was any day that Mora didn't want to walk home, it was today. Just the thought of the scary Halloween costumes, darkened skies and the freak incident in the bathroom was enough to put her on edge. As she looked upward, she noticed that the sky was peppered with a plethora of grey clouds that varied in size and shape. It reminded her of childhood cartoons where clouds would hover above characters to represent their bad luck. She wondered if it was a metaphor for her actual life given her chaotic day. The rain had lifted, but the sky was still overcast, which suggested it could resume. Daylight savings time was in full effect because dusk had arrived. It was darker than usual and had been rainy all week because of the consistent thunderstorms. She reached for her umbrella, but remembered she left it in the bathroom. She pulled her hood over her head and took her chances with the rain. She still had one reason to smile. She met a guy that showed a genuine interest in her. He was smart, compassionate, and cute. She was excited to tell, her sister, Rain the marvelous news.

Mora removed her unbroken compact mirror from her bag, but when she saw her messy hair and smeared make-up, she closed the compact and put it away. For a moment, she questioned how Edward found her attractive. It was not only her hair that bothered her, there was a small patch of discolored skin, about the size of a dime, above the left side of her lip. It happened during moments of high stress, and no matter how much skin lightening cream she used, she never replicated the even caramel skin tone she admired in her sister. She thought about calling a ride share service or a cab, but the last time she used her mother's credit card for a ride home it had erupted into a huge debacle, and she didn't want to shift the day back toward a negative trajectory. She was happy to be off that crowded bus and at one with her positive thoughts. It was not raining, and she had met Edward, and that was enough to keep her mind from drifting into the negative circumstances from earlier. She buttoned up her purple pea coat and walked home.

Mora reached the end of the sidewalk and a flash of lightning appeared across the sky. Booming thunder followed it. Its sound rattled windows and made some car alarms go off. It startled the neighborhood dogs and triggered incessant howling and loud barking. As Mora turned the corner onto the most populous street in her neighborhood, Franklin Avenue, legions of people paraded up and down the sidewalks. It was Halloween, and although it was wet outside, children were adamant and excited about trick or treating. It appeared everyone started early due to the current overcast weather. Parents held umbrellas over their children as they knocked on doors in the opulent neighborhood of Diamond Cove Estates a suburb of Potomac, Maryland. Mora's splendid memories dissipated. Every ghost costume or evil demented mask was a perpetual trigger that forced her mind toward her bathroom encounter. Telling her parents was not an option because they would not believe her. She even questioned if her supportive sister would understand. A loud blaring horn caused Mora to jump and place her hand against her heart. She looked to her left. Alongside her was a familiar vehicle driving at the pace at which she walked. The back window slowly rolled down, and a handsome man with a burgundy and grey tweed blazer hit the side of the vehicle with his hand to get her attention.

"Mora Manning," Jackson called. Mora briefly examined the individual in the car. She checked the time on her cell phone and rolled her eyes at the man in the Range Rover and kept walking.

"Young lady, I know I've raised you better than that," Jackson replied.   Mora inserted her ear buds into her ears and ignored the gentleman speaking to her. The SUV zoomed a few feet in front of her and parked. The driver, a short pudgy man with light peach-colored skin, stepped out of the car and opened the back door of the Range Rover. Out stepped a tall man with a chocolate skin tone in tailor-made slacks. He dressed immaculately. His beard was trimmed, and his hair was freshly cut. He stood in front of Mora with his hands cupped against his body and motioned for her to get in the car.

"Mora!" Jackson yelled. She stopped took out her ear buds and turned toward her father.

"What?" she asked, annoyed.

"Get in the car," he replied. Mora took off her hood and pointed to her hair and make-up.

"This is your fault. If you had arrived promptly

at 3:00 p.m., I wouldn't have bad hair and smeared make-up," Mora replied. Jackson and Mora were drawing a crowd as strangers stopped to watch their exchange, it made him uncomfortable. He loosened his tie and took a few steps closer toward his daughter.

"In the car now," countered Jackson. The increased volume and directness in his tone meant he was serious. Mora climbed in the back seat of the Range Rover, and he followed in after her. Sergio, the driver, closed the door and scurried over to the driver's side. He started the vehicle and pulled onto the road. "I'm sorry for my tardiness. I had a session run longer than expected," Jackson stated. He unbuttoned his jacket, put on his reading glasses, and picked up the business section of the newspaper.

"You're sorry all right," Mora replied. She folded her arms against her chest and blankly stared at the road. Jackson put down the paper and turned toward his daughter.

"I believe children should be able to express themselves, and that is why I allow you ample amount of latitude when speaking to me; but I will not tolerate public humiliation or disrespect. I have a reputation to uphold. If the world's number one child psychiatrist cannot handle his own daughter, it not only effects my practice but the incredible life that you live. Respect me when in public." Jackson picked back up his paper and opened up his right-side blazer pocket and took out a cigar and lighter. Mora snatched the cigar, rolled down the window, and threw it out of the car.

"Respect my lungs," Mora replied. Jackson gave his daughter an unapproving glance.

"How long are we going to fight, Mora?" Jackson asked. Mora took out her book from her backpack and started reading. Her father snatched the book and threw it in the front seat.

"How about you respect our time," Jackson retorted.

"What time? Ever since Veronica got pregnant, you have no time," Mora countered. Jackson reached in his pocket and handed her a prescription bottle.

"Aggression is one of the side effects of your latest medication so I changed your prescription, this one should calm your aggression and stop the nightmares your mother told me about," Jackson replied.

"She tells you everything. I wish she would keep some things to herself, and the medicine is not working," Mora replied.

"Are you taking it every day?" asked Jackson.

"Yes, Father. Mom blends it up in my morning

smoothie and watches me drink it." Mora grabbed the prescription bottle from her father.

"Sergio, please pass Mora the bottled water from up front?" Jackson asked. Sergio reached into the cup holder and handed it to Mora. Mora rolled her eyes, as she opened up the small white bottle, and examined the little blue pills. She placed them on her tongue, unscrewed the cap on the bottled water, and allowed the cold liquid to chase the pills down her throat. Jackson gently clutched her face between his large hands. "Open your mouth and lift your tongue," Jackson commanded. Mora obeyed her father's instruction. Jackson examined her mouth. Once there was no evidence of any medicine, he removed his hand, picked up his newspaper, and returned to reading the business section.

"And don't vomit it up, like last time," Jackson instructed. Mora handed Sergio the remaining water and sat in her seat, her arms folded across her chest. She peered out of her window at the people trick or treating with their families. She enjoyed how one little girl's father held her hand as they crossed the street. It was reminiscent of her childhood. Jackson silently observed Mora as she looked out the window. He pondered on a few words before speaking.

"Mora, I do my best given the situation with me and your mother."

"I need a dad, not a doctor," Mora responded. The bluntness of Mora's words created an invisible barrier between her and her father. Jackson sought the perfect collection of words but could not translate his feelings of inadequacy into anything that would improve the atmosphere. He reached over and rubbed Mora's hand, but as soon as she felt his touch, she balled her fist. He gently caressed it, and after a few gentle rubs, she opened up her hand and let her father hold it.

"We have arrived, Miss Mora."

"Thanks, Sergio," Mora responded. Mora gathered her belongings and waited for Sergio to open the door. As she released her father's hand and exited the vehicle, Jackson noticed that Mora had a cut on her right hand.

"What happened?" Jackson asked.

"I cut myself on my compact mirror. It's nothing really," Mora lied. Jackson reached in his pocket and took out a few hundred-dollar bills from a large wad of cash.

"Will this cover a new one?" Jackson asked. Mora gave her father a long hard looked and accepted the cash. She turned toward Sergio and placed it in his hand.

"Thank you, for opening my door," she replied.

"I can't accept this Miss Mora," Sergio replied.

"Buy your daughter Casey something memorable with it," Mora instructed.

"Thank you," he replied. Mora responded with a smile. She shook her head at her father and slammed the door.

Mora walked up the stone pathway toward her beautiful two-story home. It was a contemporary style home with lots of glass windows. In the center of the yard, was a crystal fountain the birds used as their bird bath when dry outside. Multi-colored leaves decorated the yard and chrysanthemum bushes aligned both sides of the walkway. She turned around and watched as Sergio walked back toward the SUV. Once he was in the car, Mora ran toward the back of the house. It was the only way she could ensure that she wouldn't run into her mother who would definitely punish her for having on make-up. Mora took out her key, opened the door, and entered her home. She opened the curtain next to the back door and watched as her father's black on black Range drove out of their gated community.

"He gets on my nerves," she whispered to herself. As she looked out the window, a childish girl of about eight-years old wearing a ballerina costume caught her attention. The little girl looked around to check if anybody was watching and then reached into another boy's bag and stole a handful of his candy.

She looked up and caught Mora watching her from the window. The naughty girl dropped his candy in her bag and then looked back at Mora. She raised her small hand toward her mouth and placed her index finger against her lips as a sinister grin formed across her face.

6

MY SISTER'S KEEPER

*M*ora quickly shut the curtains and jumped away from the window. A few seconds later, she gathered her courage, and reopened the curtains and searched for the girl in the ballerina costume, but she was no longer within view. Mora paused for a moment of reflection. *Am I seeing things?* The grandfather clock on the wall struck 4:00 p.m. and the loud blaring sound startled Mora. She threw her backpack down and ran up the stairs two at a time. She flicked every light switch she ran pass. She paused to catch her breath when she reached the top. *It's just a silly coincidence.* She checked her phone curious to see if Edward had called or left a text. He had not, but she did receive a couple unusual text that read, "Be quiet" followed by the number 998. Mora deleted the number but as soon as she did another text saying the same identical thing came through. She blocked the number, put her phone away and walked toward the bathroom. Mora wanted to look her best for Edward so she gathered her courage, took a deep breath, and walked in the bathroom, making sure to leave the door open. She looked in the mirror and shook her head, disgusted with what she saw. She grabbed a towel and quickly removed her runny make-up. Next, she ruffled through the drawer for her hair dryer. When she found it, she plugged it in, turned it on high, and started the arduous process of drying her hair. She combed and blow dried it simultaneously to revitalize it back to her straightened style. She thought about what she could wear and decided that she would wear a pair of tight jeans and a blouse that complimented her shoulders. Mora was fairly tall for a sixteen-year-old. She stood about 5'7" and had mocha skin. Her hair, when straightened, hung past her shoulders. She had a slim build and had an uncanny resemblance to her father. After combing her hair for several minutes, she gave up and placed the comb on the vanity.

"Why is my hair so hard to straighten!" she shouted. The lights in the bathroom flickered. Mora panicked and turned toward the bathroom door. A hooded figure stood in the doorway with its back turned toward her. "Hello, who are you?" Mora whispered. The unknown individual didn't speak. It stood in the middle of the doorway as if it wanted to block Mora from leaving the bathroom. Mora removed the hair dryer from off the counter and held it above her head. As the hooded figure turned around, Mora closed her eyes and charged toward it. The hooded figure screamed and held its hands in front of them to block Mora from attacking.

"It's me Mora! Don't hit me!" it replied. Mora stopped charging and lowered her hands to the ground when she saw who it was. Rain took out her ear buds and placed them in her pocket.

"Rain, why didn't you answer me and what's with the black hoodie?"

"I can't hear with my ear buds on high and it's wet outside. I forgot my umbrella," Rain replied.

"You scared the bejesus out of me, please no practical jokes on Halloween. You know I despise the dark," Mora replied.

"Mora, it was the thunder and lightning that caused the lights to flicker. They went off all over the house. Rain examined Mora's uncontrollable mane and walked toward the sink. Rain was the direct antithesis to her sister. She stood 5 '9" had caramel brown skin and her sandy brown hair hung to her waist. She was a fully developed eighteen-year-old who all the boys adored for all the wrong reasons. Rain walked in the bathroom and pulled some supplies from the bottom cabinet and placed them on the top of the sink. Mora enviously watched as Rain took a rubber band from one bag and pulled her hair off her neck and put it in a ponytail. She motioned for Mora to sit down on the closed toilet. Rain used a comb to part Mora's hair down the middle and applied some detangler hair solution. She held a small section and combed through it.

"What's his name," Rain asked?

"This isn't about a boy," Mora countered. Rain stopped combing her sister's hair and playfully pulled her head back and looked at her directly in the eyes.

"You have never run in the house, thrown your backpack down, and started blow drying your hair right after school. It's a boy. Now spill the tea," demanded Rain.

"He probably doesn't even like me. I mean look at my flat chest, darkened skin and bad hair, besides, he hasn't called or texted yet," Mora replied. Rain stopped combing her sister's hair and kneeled down in front of her.

"Mora you shouldn't talk down to yourself. There are plenty of girls that would love your lean frame, beautiful thick hair and mocha skin. Besides, you're only sixteen and you're still growing." Mora sighed and exhaled.

"Says the girl with caramel skin, long beautiful hair and big boobs. You and Mom don't know how it feels to look like me. Life has crowned you both with everything society deems beautiful."

"Big boobs benefit everyone, but the person who has to carry them. I gave up track because of these. But I'm making peace with my body, and you should too." Rain finished styling her sisters hair and told her to look in the mirror. Mora examined the style and shook her head.

"This look says Bora Mora. I need a look suitable for the Halloween party."

"Did he ask you to come to his Halloween party?" Rain asked, excited.

"Well... we kind of asked each other," Mora sheepishly replied.

"Go get your man, little sis," Rain joked. Rain held up her hand and Mora gave her sister a high-five.

"Stay right there; I'll be right back." Rain dashed out of the room and returned with a pair of Louboutin, a long-curled wig, and her Birkin bag. Mora jumped up with excitement and hugged her sister.

"Girl this is from the expensive side of my closet; guard these items with your life."

"Rain, I promise I will!" Mora replied, excitedly.

"If you pair this with that little black mini skirt that we bought at Bloomingdales and put in your contacts that mom doesn't know about, you will have his undivided attention. Have a seat. You can thank me later." Rain braided Mora's hair in cornrows and then adjusted the wig on her head. She took out her make-up compact and held it up in front of Mora. "This is waterproof, it's suitable for any weather." Mora sat back and watched Rain match the colors of make-up against her mocha skin. She decided upon a chocolate mocha, which was a perfect match to Mora's skin tone, but darker than Mora preferred. Mora did not complain; she decided to just enjoy the make-up session with her sister. When Rain finished, she covered Mora's eyes and led her out the bathroom so she could examine her appearance. Mora ran into her room and changed into her outfit. A few minutes later, she walked into the hallway and stood in front of Rain.

"You are beautiful, wig or no wig, make-up or no makeup. And do not let anyone tell you otherwise," Rain replied. Mora gave her sister a big hug. Rain turned Mora around and pointed her toward the mirror. Mora studied herself. For the first time in her life, she was beautiful in her own skin color. The person in front of her was not a reflection she was familiar with. She jumped up and down in excitement at her makeover. She wondered what Edward would think of her fresh look. It had taken her quite a few attempts to get her contacts in, but she succeeded and loved her face without glasses.

Mora's beautiful mocha skin glistened under her sister's new make-up. It evened her mocha tone and she was ecstatic that Rain had covered up the discolored patch of skin above her lip. She pulled her newly long hair over her shoulder. Blood red lipstick colored her perfect plump lips. The perfect shade of bronze eyeliner enhanced her beautiful brown eyes. She had on a pair of gold three-inch pumps and made sure that her Birkin bag hung perfectly in the crease where her arm met her elbow. She flipped her temporarily long luscious locks over her shoulder, pouted her red lips, and placed her hand on her hips as if she were a super model posing for the cover of a fashion magazine. Rain took the brush she was styling her hair with and held it to her mouth as if it were a microphone. "Mora Manning, you're this season's Next Supreme Model. How does it feel to be crowned the winner?" Rain asked. She extended the imaginary microphone in front of Mora's lips. Mora fanned her face with both her hands.

"It's an honor to be among the country's most beautiful women. I just want to thank the fans, the judges and everyone who helped me reach this momentous goal," Mora recited.

As she stood there, Rain watched her sister's confidence radiating. Mora flipped her long hair to the side flaunting it. A single tear fell down her cheek and Rain used a cotton ball and lightly dabbed it away.

"Don't cry Mora or you'll make me cry."

"Thank you Rain. You made me beautiful," Mora replied. Rain tilted her head back to fight her own tears.

"Don't thank me yet. We still have to get you out of the house without Mom seeing you dressed like this. You know she hates for us to wear wigs and make-up. Let me check downstairs to make sure the coast is clear," Rain replied.

7

THE INCIDENT

*R*ain held up her hand and motioned for Mora to stay upstairs. She took off her shoes, not wanting to make a sound as she sauntered down the stairs. When she reached the bottom, she walked through the kitchen and peeked down the hallway. Their mother, Mary Anne, was sitting on the bed folding clothes. The coast was clear. Mora watched from upstairs and waited impatiently for the signal from Rain. Rain ran toward the staircase and signaled for Mora to come down the steps. Mora took one foot and placed it on the step. She tried her darndest to be as discreet as possible and to make no sound, but the heels were making too much noise. Mora took off the shoes and held them against her chest. But as she descended the stairs, one shoe fell out of her hand and made a loud clanking sound as it tumbled down the stairs. A voluptuous woman with a caramel skin tone came walking into the living room. She stood about 5'8" and had her hair swooped into a ponytail that hung abundantly down her back. When Rain saw her mother coming toward her, she motioned for Mora to run back upstairs, but it was too late. Mary Anne had seen Mora provocatively dressed. She glanced at Mora and then looked at Rain and placed both of her hands on her hips.

"Where do you think you are going dressed like that?" Mary Anne snapped.

"I'm just going to a Halloween party," Mora replied her eyes looking down at the ground.

"Will there be adult supervision?" Mary Anne probed.

"I don't know, it's just some kids from school," Mora replied.

"Oh, so it is a little boy that has you dressing provocative," Mary Anne responded. Rain stood between Mora and her mother and interrupted the conversation.

"Mom, she's sixteen and it's just a little make-up and a wig. Everybody wears make-up and extensions. It is not every day. I get to give my little sister a make-over," responded Rain.

Mary Anne turned her head toward Rain. Her brown eyes pierced into her like laser beams, but she did not say a word. She walked over to the kitchen counter and snatched a paper towel from the roller, ran it under some hot water, and grabbed Mora's chin and tried to remove the make-up off her face. Mora pushed her mother away from her and turned her face from left to right in an attempt to keep her from destroying her beautiful make-up. She tried to run away, but Mary Anne had a powerful grip on her face.

"Little girl, you think I'm going to let you get away with putting your hands on me?" Mary Anne questioned.

"Stop, Mom! You are messing it up!" Mora yelled. Mary Anne snatched the purse from Mora and threw it across the room. Mora's phone fell out along with a few other contents. She pulled the long wig off Mora's head and threw it to the ground. Anger grew in Mora and her blood boiled beneath her veins. Her fingers balled into a fist. She stared at her mother straight in the eye and let out a loud and bellowing scream.

"I hate you!" Mora yelled. She stomped up the stairs and slammed the door. Rain walked toward her mother and looked her straight in the eye.

"Mom, it's just a little hair and make-up," Rain stated.

"I'm a single parent raising two teenage girls without the assistance of their father. I refuse to allow my daughters to dress like skanks. You know the rules, no make-up, wigs or provocative clothing until eighteen," Mary Anne barked. She picked up Mora's phone to put in back in the purse and it rang. Mary Anne looked at the screen and there was an incoming call from, "Chocolate dimples." Rain tried to grab the phone from her mother but was unsuccessful.

"Mom; don't answer her phone. That's an invasion of her privacy," Rain replied.

"I pay this phone bill and there is no privacy in this house unless you are in the bathroom," Mary Anne replied. She pressed the accept button and put the phone to her ear.

"Hello who is chocolate dimples," Mary Anne replied.

"Chocolate dimples? Is this Mora's phone?" Edward asked.

"Yes, this is her mother, what's your name young man and don't tell me chocolate dimples is your rap name." Rain puts her head in her hands, embarrassed for her sister.

"My name is Edward and I don't listen to rap,"

Edward chuckled. "It's nice to meet you Mrs. Manning. Can I speak to Mora?"

"Mora is unavailable and won't be able to attend your party," she replied.

"I'm sorry to hear that, is she okay?"

"She's fine," Mary Anne replied.

"Could you tell her to call me when......" Mary Anne hung up the phone, powered it off and threw it on the kitchen counter.

"Mom, that was absolutely uncalled for," Rain yelled.

"No, what's uncalled for is my daughter telling me she hates me." He's bad news. You should have heard him on the phone being extra polite as if I can't see through that façade." Mary Anne headed upstairs to give Mora a piece of her mind, but Rain ran in front of her and blocked her from going upstairs.

"Please, let me talk to her," Rain pleaded. Mary Anne pondered Rain's suggestion, and after she thought about it, she agreed. Rain ran upstairs after her sister and lightly knocked against the bathroom door.

"Go away!" Mora yelled.

"It's me, Mora," Rain replied

"I don't want to talk; I want to be alone," Mora replied. Rain leaned against the door and waited a few minutes. She searched for words that would soothe her sister's anger.

"Mora, I 'm sorry Mom ruined your day. Maybe when we visit Dad, we can do another make-up session, when Mom is not around?" suggested Rain. Rain waited for a response, but when she didn't receive one, she leaned her head against the door. The sound of Mora's whimpering in the bathroom caused her to hurt with her sister. She glanced at her watch. It was almost 6:00 p.m. and she was late for her Halloween party. A genius idea popped in her head. She ran down the steps and walked into the dining room. Her mom was having her afternoon tea and reading a hair magazine.

"Mom, can Mora go with me to my party? I'd watch her," Rain asked.

"Absolutely not. She has an anger problem, and she needs to sit upstairs and think about what she said. I will not reward disobedience."

"I spent hours building up her-self-esteem, and you tore it down in seconds," Rain added.

"My house. My rules. If you don't like it, get out," Mary Anne commanded. Rain walked over to the closet and snatched her jacket from off the hanger. She picked up her shoes next to the stairs, and slammed the door. Mary Anne rose from the table and walked to the front of the house to reprimand

Rain, but it was too late. She was already in her car backing out of the driveway when she reached the door.

"I'll deal with her when she returns," Mary Anne whispered to herself. She walked to the dining room table and continued to sip on her tea while she perused various hair magazines. She was in search of a new style for her client. After a few moments of silence, a cloud of guilt descended upon her. She wondered if she handled the situation with Mora a little too harshly. She released a lengthy sigh and headed upstairs to apologize to her daughter. When she reached the top of the stairs, Mora was standing there with her arms folded across her chest.

"You let Rain go to her party, but I can't go to mine?" Mora questioned.

"Mora, I will deal with Rain when she returns. Put on your little Red Riding Hood costume and let's go trick or treating before it's too late," Mary Anne instructed.

"Mom, what sixteen-year-old trick or treats with their mother?" Mora replied. Mary Anne walked up the stairs, but Mora moved to the left and blocked her from going any further.

"Mora, step aside and let me upstairs." Mora stood on the stairs and ignored her mother. As Mary Anne moved to the right, Mora shifted her meager frame to the right to block her mother from her desired destination. Mary Anne grasped Mora by her wrist, but Mora had the upper hand being on the top step and was stronger than she thought. She snatched her wrist from her mother, and Mary Anne lost her balance. Her eyes widened, and her hands grasped the air for anything that would keep her from falling. She reached her hand out to Mora, but Mora took a step backwards onto the top stair to keep from falling with her mother. As a result, Mary Anne tumbled down the lengthy flight of marble stairs.

Mora watched as her mother hit her head on one step after the other until she reached the bottom. She laid at the bottom of the stairs motionless. For a brief moment, Mora felt justice had been served and was happy her mother received what she deserved. But her tune quickly changed when blood dripped out of the right side of Mary Anne's forehead and onto the floor. Mora ran down the steps, got on her knees, and checked her mother's pulse. She was still breathing. She jumped up and dug through her mother's purse until she found her mother's phone. Mora dialed 9... 1..., but before she pressed the last 1, her mother gripped her ankle. Mora screamed and shook her leg to wiggle herself loose, but Mary Anne had a firm grip and refused to release her. She yanked Mora's leg, and she fell to the ground.

"What the hell is wrong with you? You let me fall down the stairs!" Mary Anne yelled. She lifted herself from off the ground and touched the side of her head. Her caramel fingers had spots of blood on them. She cut Mora an ugly glance and walked out of the living room. Mora knew that look and it meant trouble. She searched for a hiding space, but it was too late. A few seconds later, Mary Anne returned with a belt in one hand and a towel covering her head in the other. Mary Anne pulled her arm back and whipped that belt forward.

"Get over here little girl!" Mary Anne demanded. Mora sprinted up the stairs, determined to not get a whipping from her mother.

Mary Anne swung the belt at Mora but missed her by a fraction of an inch. Mora ran into the bathroom, slammed the door, and locked it. Mary Anne ran to the upstairs bathroom door and repeatedly banged on the door.

"Open up the damn door, Mora!" Mary Anne yelled.

"Leave me alone or I will call Child Protective Services." Mary Anne paused and leaned against the door.

"Not without your cell phone." Mora remembered that the contents of her purse had fallen out earlier. She kicked the cabinet sink, annoyed. Mary

Anne knocked on the door with her fist. "You have to come out eventually, missy, and when you do me and my belt will be waiting." Mary Anne waited a few seconds for Mora to open the door, but a knock at the front door caught her attention. She looked in the hall mirror, wiped a few drops of blood from her face, and headed downstairs.

8

REFLECTION

*A*n injured Mary Anne placed both hands on the marble railings. She sauntered down the stairs as if she were a toddler discovering steps for the first time. Once she had made it to the bottom of the steps, she limped toward the door. The throbbing in her leg caused her to pause. She lifted her pants leg and underneath was a nasty discolored blue and reddish bruise on the inside of her right calf. She touched it slightly and intense pain shot through her body. The aftereffects of the fall were worse than she thought. She pulled down her pant leg and limped to the door. She looked in the peephole, smiled, and opened the door.

"Trick or treat," replied the small group of children who were escorted by a tall man in a clown costume. She grabbed the candy bowl with delectable treats off the end table and placed handfuls into each child's orange pumpkin bucket. Once she finished handing out the candy, she wished them a happy evening and closed the door. She went into the bathroom medicine cabinet and took some ibuprofen and washed it down with a bottle of water from the fridge. She searched the freezer for an ice pack and when she found it placed it against her head, and had a seat on the couch. While sitting there she saw a picture hanging of herself, Mora, Rain and Jackson on the wall. She stared at the picture and reminisced on the past. She wished they were still a happy family and she did not have to raise two teenage girls alone. *If only Jackson would return.* A single tear fell from her eye as she pondered how to handle the situation with Mora.

Mora paced back and forth in the spacious bathroom. She walked toward the window, lifted it up, and checked the distance between the second floor and the ground. If she jumped, she would not make it without severely injuring herself. "Help, someone! Please help me!" The blaring horns, sporadic rain and laughter of the trick or treaters were too much noise for her to compete with. Mora slammed the window shut, walked over to the door, and pulled it to ensure it was locked. She pressed her ear against it to see if she could hear her mother on the other side.

She contemplated opening the door to run and grab her tablet from her room. If she could connect to the internet, she could call Rain or her father to keep her mother from whipping her. She did not want to take that chance and decided she would wait in the bathroom until Rain returned home. At least then she would have someone who could be a buffer between her and her mother.

Mora sat on the edge of the bathroom tub and pondered what she could do to pass the time. Directly across from the tub was an oversized oval mirror above the sink. It stood about four feet tall. Out of the corner of Mora's eye, she saw the mirror, and turned away. She regretted her decision to lock herself in the bathroom, but she really did not have another option. Her bedroom door was absent a lock, courtesy of her mother. It was too quiet now. There were no honking horns, and no chatter of pedestrians. The only sound she heard was the rustle of the wind shrilling through the trees.

Mora re-opened the window. Silence was her enemy. The loud noise distracted her from her fearful and worrisome thoughts. Her contacts irritated her eyes, so she removed them and put on her purple glasses she left in the left drawer of the cabinet. She scrubbed the make-up from her face. No matter how hard she scrubbed or how much soap she used, the make-up was not coming off fast enough. She scrubbed harder, but to no avail. Frustrated, Mora threw the towel into the sink which resulted in splashes of water falling all over the floor. The lights flickered off and Mora immediately panicked. Faint whispers uttered Mora's name. She tried to avoid looking in the mirror, but she could see those red demon-like eyes out of the corner of her eye. They shot through the dark like lasers as they peered directly at her. When she looked up, there in the mirror stood the demented ghost like reflection with a sadistic grin on it's face. It just stood there as if it had all the time in the world.

It was identical to the one she had seen a few hours ago. It moved its neck in an erratic and distorted way. Mora dashed toward the bathroom door and unlocked it. She pulled the doorknob, but the door would not open. She wrapped both her hands on the doorknob and yanked it repeatedly, it was stuck. No matter how hard she pulled, it would not budge. "Mom, open the door! I'm stuck!" she yelled. Her mother did not come. She banged on the door and frequently looked behind her. The bathroom window slammed shut, and the glass shattered. The light bulbs in the bathroom popped and made Mora jump. The drawers and cabinets in the bathroom began opening and closing repeatedly as if being controlled by some unseen force. Darkness strangled the light and lingered in the crevices of the bathroom walls. Only a slight glimmer of light from the streetlamp outside the window shined into the bathroom. An incessant raspy child-like voice chanted a haunting phrase.

"Sticks and stones rarely break bones, but your actions will make me harm you," it roared.

"Why do you keep tormenting me?" Mora screamed, with a quiver in her voice. Chill bumps traveled from Mora's feet all the way to the top of her head. Her heartbeat increased. Mora opened her mouth to scream, but it was as if something muted her voice. Worried, she touched her throat and screamed again, but again there was no sound. She pounded on the door. The temperature in the bathroom plummeted. Mora could see her breath. A slow cracking sound caused Mora to turn around. Miniature pieces of glass fell from the mirror and spilled over into the sink and onto the floor. The crack in the mirror continued to widen as two fluid-like oil-colored hands protruded through the glass. Its fingers grasped the air like they were reaching for something.

Inch by inch, the hands and fingers pressed through the mirror until the forearms were visible. Its yellow crystallized fingernails moved like impatient spiders as they tapped the top of the ceramic vanity.

The sound they created resembled that of long nails tapping a glass tabletop. They left remnants of their oily residue after every touch. Next, the shoulders and a head protruded forth from out of the mirror. Large shards of glass fell to the floor. Mora pushed her body close to the door. She opened her mouth to scream, but again no sound came forth. The repetitive clicking sound returned. It caused her to turn around, and she watched as the reflection gripped its large oily hands on the edge of the vanity and pulled itself from out of the mirror. Once it had pulled itself from out of the mirror, it sat quietly on top of the vanity. Without advanced notice, it pounced on the floor and landed on all fours like a black cat but with one hundred times it's force. *Click... click... click... click...* was the sound the reflection's neck made when it turned its head toward Mora. It lifted one of its oil-laden fingers and motioned for Mora to come toward it. Mora beat her fist against the door. The reflection crawled toward Mora. Its yellow fingernails clawed against the ceramic tile floor. At the faintest touch, the ceramic cracked. The sound it produced resembled fingernails scratching against a chalkboard as the long crystal-like nails dragged across the floor. The reflections red eye's followed Mora's every move. Mora pulled on the door with all her might and frequently checked how close the reflection was to her. Every time she looked, the reflection was getting closer and closer toward her.

The reflection was in arms reach, it lunged at her ankles. Its nails anchored themselves into her skin and yanked Mora to the ground. Mora held onto the doorknob as long as she could, but the force from the reflection was too strong. She released the doorknob and fell to the floor. The reflection's fluid-like fingers lengthened and wrapped themselves around Mora's legs similar to how a spider would cocoon their developing egg. It dragged her toward the mirror. Mora clawed for anything she could to keep from being taken by the reflection. Her small fingers grasped the shower curtain and yanked down the curtain rod. She struggled to wrap her hand around the rod, but when she did, she shoved the long metal pole into the reflection's stomach, and Mora immediately felt a hard push in her own stomach. The reflection girl hissed, then jumped on top of Mora and pinned her to the ground by her wrist.

"Tell me I'm pretty, tell me I'm pretty!" the reflection girl yelled, in her wicked child-like tone. Tears fell from Mora's eyes and onto the frames of her glasses which made it hard for her to see. The reflection girl increased the pressure she applied to Mora's wrist. It pressed the full weight of its body against her paltry physique. "Tell me I'm pretty," it uttered again and again as it waited for a response, but all Mora could do was move her lips. She released Mora's hands, threw her over her shoulder, and leaped on top of the vanity in a single jump.

She extended her hands over the broken glass and the fragmented pieces rose from the ground like nails would to a magnet. They reassembled themselves within the mirror. It pressed its left hand through the glass, but his time it did not crack. It swirled as if it were a portal. When Mora saw the swirling vortex, she feared for her life. She gathered all the strength she could muster and bit the reflection girl on the shoulder. Its skin wasn't hard like ceramic as she previously thought. It tasted leathery, a little tougher than human flesh. Mora and the reflection girl both screamed. Her screams broke through the forced silence. The volume of their collective voices echoed throughout the house. Mora's pain was so intense that she faded in and out of consciousness. Mary Anne ran from downstairs to the upstairs bathroom in record time. She turned the doorknob, but it would not budge.

"Mora, open the door!" Mary Anne yelled. When there was no response, Mary Anne ran into the kitchen, grabbed a butter knife, and sprinted up the stairs two at a time. She fidgeted with the lock. The reflection girl heard the doorknob rattle and emitted a loud hissing sound. She threw Mora to the floor and retreated into the mirror. The lights came back on, the fluid like mirror returned to solid glass, the curtain rod attached itself back to the wall, the glass from the window reassembled itself and the open cabinets and drawers closed. The bathroom looked like no incident ever occurred and was perfectly intact. A frantic Mary Anne burst through the door where Mora laid severely injured in her own blood. Mary Anne screamed and fell to the floor. She snatched a large bath towel from the towel rack and wrapped her daughter in it. She lifted Mora off the ground and guided her to the car, their destination the hospital.

9

QUESTIONS AND ANSWERS

*M*ary Anne opened the back door of her car and placed Mora inside. Sizeable amounts of blood seeped through the white terry cloth towel that was wrapped around Mora's body. She sat in a fetal position in the back of the car with her hands wrapped tightly around her legs. Her teeth chattered as she looked blankly out the front window as she rocked back and forth. She was in a state of shock. When she saw the rearview and side mirrors, she buried her face into her knees, frightened that the reflection girl might appear again. Mary Anne started the car, and the ignition sputtered---a *click, click, clicking* sound. Mora lifted her head, covered her ears, and searched around the car for the source of the sound. "She's everywhere! I can hear her!" Mora yelled. Mora scooted behind the seat of her mother. She wrapped her arms in a death grip around her mother's neck. Mary Anne, unable to breathe, tried to pull Mora's arm from around her neck, and after some struggling, succeeded.

"Who's going to get you Mora?" Mary Anne asked, breathless. Mary Anne took her hands off of the steering wheel and rubbed her hands up and down Mora's arms. The coldness of Mora's body shocked her. Mary Anne took one hand and turned the key in the ignition. The car started. She then turned the dial on the heat to provide her daughter some warmth. "Take a deep breath, everything will be fine." Mora loosened her grip and after a few moments settled back into her seat. She clicked the lock button on her passenger side door and all the doors locked. Mary Anne put the car in reverse, and once she was out of her gated subdivision, she floored the accelerator and sped to the closest hospital. Concern, worry, and fear were the unspoken emotions that caused Mary Anne to perform rolling stops and honk her horn at nearby vehicles as she sought to get her daughter the help she needed. Mora covered her eyes and laid her head in her lap. Every few moments, Mary Anne reached over and caressed her daughter's hand. "Mora, you want to discuss what happened in the bathroom darling?" she asked, worried. Mora kept her head facing toward the floor and did not speak.

Mary Anne decided to leave the topic alone. She did not want to make matters worse by triggering something that would cause her daughter to react in an uncontrollable way. Mary Anne looked in the rearview mirror. She noticed Mora had lifted her head. Snot ran down her nose, and her towel was getting bloodier by the minute. Mora moved closer toward the back of the driver's seat. She leaned forward and whispered in her mother's ear.

"Do you remember the hush ghost that appeared in my dreams?" Mora whispered.

"Yes, Mora, I remember."

"She tried to pull me into the bathroom mirror," Mora whispered.

"Who tried to pull you into the mirror?" Mary Anne asked.

"The hush ghost!" Mora yelled. Mary Anne remained expressionless. This was more severe than she imagined. She looked up and saw the sign, Valley Memorial Hospital. As she drove toward the building, memories detailing her own encounters with hospitals surfaced. Mary Anne did not want to turn right into the hospital parking lot, but Mora's mental and physical wellbeing depended upon it. She chose a space that was closest to the primary entrance.

Mary Anne jumped out of the car and opened Mora's door. As she helped her out of the car, she looked Mora in the eye and held Mora's hand.

"If you repeat what you shared with me in the car, they will take you away from us and I don't know what I would do if someone took you from me."

"She's getting stronger, and she will get me. Why won't you believe me?" Mora cried. She dropped her head into her hand and let the tears fall freely from her eyes. Mary Anne wrapped Mora in the towel and got a better glimpse of the cuts and lacerations on Mora's body. The puncture wounds and the scratches all along her arms from the broken glass alarmed Mary Anne. Mora and Mary Anne's eyes met.

"Do you think I would harm myself?" Mora asked. Mary Anne shifted her eyes to Mora's wounds and took the towel and swathed it around her arm.

"Let's get someone to examine these," she replied. Mary Anne helped Mora out of the car. Mora put her left arm around her mother's neck. They both limped toward the emergency room doors. The rain started again; its drops sounded like minia-ture drums as they beat against the pavement. Mary Anne was moving so fast she almost fell in a small pothole filled with water. Her hair and clothes were wet. She was out of breath from the stress of carrying

Mora's bodyweight coupled with her own. As they power walked toward the hospital doors, she noticed that Mora's pace was slowing. She looked at her daughter and saw her eyes roll back in her head and a stream of blood running down her leg. She felt the pull of Mora's body falling to the ground. Adrenaline surged through Mary Anne's body, and with a strength she did not know existed, she picked Mora up and ran through the automatic doors. Once inside, she stood at the front of the emergency waiting room and yelled.

"Somebody, anybody, help my daughter!" Her voice traveled throughout the waiting room and startled a few of the patients. An infant child cried, and a small little boy dropped his sippy cup on the ground. One man shielded his young daughter's face so she would not have nightmares about Mary Anne and Mora's appearance. Drops of bloody water dripped from both their clothing. Mary Anne and Mora looked as if they had just stepped off the set of a horror movie. The middle-aged receptionist with streaks of grey in her hair at the front desk, put down her sandwich and picked up the phone when Mary Anne and Mora came through the door. This was not the hospital in which their primary physician practiced, but it was the one closest to their home. A male nurse came running with a gurney and took Mora from Mary Anne's arms.

"What happened to her?" he said, shocked as he examined the cuts on her arms and puncture wounds on her legs. He leaned Mora against the gurney to relieve Mary Anne of the burden of Mora's weight. She searched for the correct set of words that would allow her to explain the situation without her or Mora appearing crazy. After a short awkward silence, she pushed forth an answer.

"I heard her screaming. When I found her, she was barely conscious in puddles of her blood." The nurse had more questions, but decided he would let a licensed physician continue the probing. He waved for another nurse's help, and they both lifted Mora on the gurney and rushed it down the long hallway. Mary Anne followed closely behind, but when she reached the emergency room doors that said for personnel only, one of the male nurses stopped and turned toward her.

"We will take it from here," he replied. Mary Anne did not argue. She did what she was told. She nervously bit her nails and had a seat on one of the chairs. Her teeth chattered. She wrapped her arms around her body to keep herself warm. She was in an urgent hurry and did not grab a jacket. Mary Anne surveyed the room, and several patrons in the hospital stared at her. It made her uncomfortable. *Is it my guilt or are they silently judging me?* Mary Anne stood up and paced up and down the foyer as she waited for a report of her daughter's wellbeing. Her clothes were wet and dripping bloody water all over the floor. The middle-aged woman with a creamy vanilla skin tone who phoned the nurses when Mary Anne and Mora walked in, waved at Mary Anne to get her attention.

"Miss! Miss!" she uttered. Mary Anne, preoccupied with her own thoughts, did not pay the woman any attention. The receptionist stood up, walked from behind the desk, and tapped Mary Anne on the shoulder. Her unexpected tap caused Mary Anne to jump and almost bump into another young lady sitting not too far from where she stood.

"I'm so sorry," she replied. The young woman moved to another seat across the aisle. The receptionist handed Mary Anne a clean smock, an ice pack, and a towel.

"You should freshen up; the bathroom's straight ahead," the receptionist said. Mary Anne looked down at her blouse. It was ripped, had spots of blood and one of her buttons were undone.

"Thank you," Mary Anne replied. Mary Anne looked behind her and noticed a trail of light-red water that a janitor was mopping up. She nodded to the gentleman, in appreciation. He responded with a grimacing scowl and continued picking up the water while placing down yellow caution signs. Mary Anne headed to the bathroom. To calm herself, she inhaled and exhaled long slow deep breaths. Slow, meditative style breathing always relaxed her. Once inside the restroom, she wiped traces of blood from her face and hands. She examined herself in the mirror. The blood from her head injury, had dripped down her face, neck and onto her blouse. *No wonder everyone was staring,* she thought. Mary Anne placed both her hands on the side of the sink, and streams of tears flowed from her eyes.

"It's all my fault," she uttered. The acoustics in the bathroom caused her words to reverberate. She ran warm water over the towel and wiped the blood from her face. Every few washes, she rung out the towel's excess water and watched the red colored water drip into the sink. With every rinse, the water from the towel became clearer. *If only our pain and hurt was this easy to cleanse,* she thought. Her tears and her daughter's blood mingled together and circled down the drain. Mary Anne wiped her nose, changed her shirt and checked her appearance in the mirror. She wrapped her soiled blouse in the towel and headed back to the waiting room. When she returned, the receptionist handed her a clip board with a few forms to fill out regarding Mora and her medical history. The receptionist placed her hand on top of Mary Anne's to offer solace.

"It will be okay," she said. Mary Anne appreciated the woman's kind gesture but wondered why she would make such statements after seeing the condition of her daughter. She took a seat along the back wall as far away from the other patients as possible. She regretted what she had to do next, call Jackson. They agreed they would always keep each other abreast on any life-threatening situation involving their daughters regardless of how they felt about each other. The last thing she needed was his judgement coupled with her guilt. She did not have a choice, she had to call. She fished in her purse for her phone and scrolled through her contacts until she found Jackson's number. She took a deep breath, dialed the number, and placed the receiver to her ear.

"Hello, Mary Anne," Jackson answered. Mary Anne searched for the correct words that would inform but not worry Jackson. "Mary Anne is everything okay?"

"Mora and I are at Valley Memorial Hospital. She had an accident," replied Mary Anne.

"I just dropped her off a few hours ago, what happened?" Jackson questioned.

"I'll explain everything when you get here. Just hurry and leave Veronica at the house."

Mary Anne hung up the phone and picked up a magazine on the seat next to her. She flipped through the pages to pass the time while she silently dreaded the impending conversation she had to have with Jackson. She prayed that he did not bring Veronica, because she did not have the desire or patience to listen to her unwelcomed critiques about how she should raise her daughters.

10

JACKSON

*J*ackson Manning arrived at Valley Memorial Hospital impeccably dressed. He sported a crème colored blazer and a fine pair of tailored grey trousers paired with cream colored snakeskin boots. Every time he walked into a room, everyone took notice of his broad chest and tall stature. He tipped his fedora hat to a few women in the room as his eyes skimmed the room for his ex-wife, Mary Anne. On his arm was his fiancée Veronica Child. She was a slender built woman with a glowing chocolate skin tone. Her skin was flawless. It appeared as if she were wearing make-up, although she rarely did. Veronica always dressed in the latest and most fashionable designer clothes from head to toe. Today that was comprised of a white mink coat, a black fitted Dolce and

Gabbana dress that hugged her in just the right places and three-inch heels. Her long jet-black hair hung down her back in loose curls. She smacked on chewing gum and ran her hand over her yellow diamond amulet necklace, almost as if she were silently boasting. Jackson took the umbrella that was covering both of them and placed it in the corner by the vending machine for it to dry. Veronica placed her hand on her barely there pregnant stomach and clung to Jackson's left arm like white on rice. Every few seconds she fanned herself as if she were hot to make sure that everyone got a glimpse of her new three-carat diamond engagement ring. Jackson found Mary Anne sitting in the corner filling out paperwork. He rushed toward her. Veronica followed not too far behind him. Jackson lightly tapped her shoulder, and when Mary Anne saw him, she was overwhelmed with emotion and hugged him at once. Jackson, not wanting to be rude, hugged her but quickly stepped away.

"How's Mora?" Jackson asked.

"I haven't received an update; but she was bleeding pretty bad...," Mary Anne stopped in mid-sentence when she saw Veronica. Jackson knew by the scowl on Mary Anne's face as she noticed Veronica's presence that he needed to act fast. He stood up and whispered something in Veronica's ear. Veronica pushed her gold bangles up her arm and folded her hands across her perky breast. She pouted her lips and analyzed Mary Anne's appearance. Her homely attire, and horrible fashion bothered her. She wondered how Jackson had ever been enthralled by such mediocrity. Veronica turned her back toward Mary Anne and headed to the coffee stand. She swung her hips, twirled her hair, and mumbled something under her breath. Once Veronica was out of view, Mary Anne turned toward Jackson.

"Why did you bring her here after I specifically asked you not to?" Mary Anne questioned. Jackson stepped closer toward Mary Anne. He brought the volume of his thick southern accent down to a whisper.

"Mary Anne, we have discussed this, she has a right to be here," Jackson responded.

"Your whore needs to go. I can't deal with her unwelcomed judgment *and* focus on the health of my daughter at the same time."

"Veronica is my fiancée and soon to be wife. Make peace with this, Mary Anne," replied Jackson. Mary Anne rose from out of her seat and stared Jackson straight in the eye.

"No, she's the slut you cheated on me with which resulted in the dissolution of our marriage!" Mary Anne put her hand against her head then stumbled to the left. Jackson caught her before she fell. He slowly helped her regain her balance by placing one of his strong, masculine hands on the small of her back. For a split second, they both gazed into each other's eyes until a slight drop of blood broke Jackson's attention on Mary Anne's forehead.

"What happened to you? Are you okay?" Jackson asked.

"I'm fine. I just fell down the steps trying to get to Mora in time," Mary Anne replied.

"You fell down the stairs?" Jackson questioned. Mary Anne nodded. He held her hand and guided her into her seat. She leaned forward to pick up the ice pack and towel on the table, but Jackson reached out his hand and grabbed it for her. He put the ice pack in the empty seat to his left, then leaned her head toward him. Mary Anne wanted to resist, but the warmness of his hands, and the gentleness of his touch against her body was the comfort she needed during this tumultuous time. He patted her cut with the partially wet towel and absorbed the small dribbles of blood. Once finished, he examined her head.

"It's a shallow cut. It will heal on its own. Just keep your head elevated," Jackson commanded. Mary Anne followed his suggestion and lifted her chin a little higher. Jackson slowly took the ice pack from her head and handed it to her.

"Veronica will return at any moment," Jackson responded. She placed the ice pack on her own head and gave Jackson a disapproving glance.

"Now, what exactly happened with Mora?" he asked.

"It upset her when I wouldn't let her wear make-up and a wig to some boy's unsupervised Halloween party. That's what started it. Next thing I know she's screaming in the upstairs bathroom. I had to use a knife to pry the door open. When I found her, she was barely conscious and laying on the floor in remnants of her blood."

"This is about a boy and a Halloween costume? You should have just let her go. For God's sake she's sixteen Mary Anne."

"No, it's not just about a boy and a Halloween costume. It's about my sixteen-year-old dressing like a twenty-one-year-old at an unsupervised party with horny teenage boys!" Mary Anne disputed. Mary Anne and Jackson's heated arguments started to draw attention from the patients in the hospital. Jackson lowered his tone in hopes that Mary Anne would do the same.

"I'm sorry; I didn't mean to criticize your parenting skills," Jackson responded. Mary Anne turned her back toward Jackson. She hated for anyone, especially him, to witness her onslaught of tears.

"I drove her to the hospital and called you as soon as I arrived." She lifted her head back to keep her tears from running down her cheeks. Jackson held her hand and caressed it. His accusatory words hurt her. He realized that this incident had been emotionally challenging for Mary Anne and that he needed to be supportive in this time of need. Mary Anne laid her head on Jackson's shoulder. She was thankful that she was not alone. His training as a physician taught him how to remain calm in dire situations. It was one of his qualities she admired most. Mary Anne looked up and saw Veronica walking with a cup holder. She released his hand and spoke to him in a soft yet commanding voice.

"Tell Veronica to leave," she instructed.

"She was with me when you called."

"Miss America can sit her prissy ass in the car," Mary Anne countered. Jackson was about to speak, but Veronica had now returned with three cups of coffee. She stood there silently and tapped her foot against the floor while she stared at the both of them. Once the hint registered, Jackson jumped up and removed the coffee from Veronica's hands. She leaned her head to the left, and he kissed her on the cheek. Mary Anne held her anger inside and kindly accepted her coffee from Jackson.

"Did you happen to grab any cream or sugar?" she asked.

"I'm sorry; I didn't think someone of your size would want to overindulge in empty calories. Have you tried it black? It's strong, an appetite suppressant, and will give you plenty of energy, and it was Miss Universe, my dear."

"What do you mean with my size, I'm a size eight," Mary Anne jabbed.

"That's not something; I'd go around advertising my dear," Veronica whispered. Veronica pulled a disinfectant wipe from her purse and thoroughly cleaned the chair she was about to sit in. She crossed her legs, perused the used magazines until she found one to her liking, and sipped her black cold brew through a metal straw. She noticed that Mary Anne's eyes were red. She handed her a couple of tissues. Mary Anne did not want to accept the tissue but did so anyway. She refused to let Veronica know her comment had upset her. Mary Anne dabbed the pink perfume scented tissues underneath her eyes. Veronica leaned forward and placed her hand on Mary Anne's knee. "I can't have you sitting in my company; with those puffy red eyes; pull yourself together my dear. You've garnered quite the audience. Now, how is our daughter, Mora?"

questioned Veronica. Mary Anne moved her knee from under Veronica's hand which caused Veronica's coffee to spill all over her dress. Veronica gripped the chair to keep herself from falling face down to the floor. Mary Anne let out a light chuckle.

"Karma's a bitch, isn't she?" Mary Anne asked. Veronica took out a white linen cloth from her purse and dabbed at the spilled coffee on her dress.

"Dresses are replaceable, but husbands are not," she replied. She turned toward Jackson placed both of her hands against his face and pressed her ruby red lips against his. Jackson wanted to resist but always found it difficult to withstand Veronica's charm. He returned the kiss then quickly grabbed Veronica's hands from off of his face and escorted her toward the other side of the waiting room. He could since the tension between the two ladies escalating and wanted to put a stop to it before they became more of a spectacle than they already were. Mary Anne turned away so she would not have to witness the man she still loved kiss another woman. Jackson mouthed that he was sorry to Mary Anne, picked up the umbrella by the side of the vending machine and walked Veronica out of the hospital.

A few moments later, a pudgy fellow with a thick mustache and vanilla-hued skin walked in the waiting room holding a metal clipboard in his hand. He examined the now semi-crowded room before calling the next name on his list. "Mary Anne Manning," he called. Mary Anne stood up and waved her hand and walked in his direction. When he spotted her, he walked toward her and met her in front of the receptionist's desk. Mary Anne was apprehensive about hearing the news regarding Mora. Jackson reached Mary Anne, and the gentleman at precisely the right time.

"I'm Dr. Moseley, Mora's presiding physician," he greeted.

"I'm Dr. Manning," Jackson responded.

"How's Mora?" Mary Anne asked.

"She is in stable condition, but we had to do an emergency blood transfusion." Mary Anne put both of her hands over her mouth. Jackson placed his arm around Mary Anne's waist and brought her closer. I am concerned about her injuries, especially the cuts and lacerations on her arms and legs.

"Lacerations?" Jackson questioned.

"Does Mora have any history of harming herself?"

"No, she's never harmed herself," Mary Anne responded.

"Have you been physical with her?" Dr. Moseley

continued. Mary Anne folded her arms across her chest.

"We don't beat our children, if that's what you're suggesting," Mary Anne snapped.

"These questions are just formalities; I am not accusing you of anything, Mrs. Manning."

"When can we see Mora?" Jackson interrupted.

"She's resting, but I don't see anything wrong with you seeing her. I would also like to keep Mora here for the next 72 hours."

"Why?" Mary Anne asked.

"I'm concerned about the troubling things she said as she went in and out of consciousness and after examining her wounds and lacerations, I believe she could be a danger to herself," Dr. Moseley answered.

"Troubling things?" Jackson questioned.

"She just kept mumbling about being harmed," Dr. Moseley responded.

"Mora has a vivid imagination and reads horror novels; you can't take the things she says so literally," Mary Anne replied.

"I'm sorry, Mrs. Manning. We take these things very seriously."

"Please take us to see her," Jackson interrupted.

"Follow me," Dr. Moseley replied. He led them through the emergency room doors to where their daughter Mora was resting.

11

BROKEN

*D*r. Moseley, Mary Anne, and Jackson headed down a weakly illumined hallway. The culprit, a bulb that flickered intermittently in the north corridor. Dr. Moseley stopped one custodian and pointed toward the bulb. The young man smiled and gave Dr. Moseley a thumbs up. Tiny chill bumps formed on Mary Anne's arm. She rubbed her hands over her arms to keep warm. Jackson removed his blazer and placed it over her shoulders. She placed her hands in the arms of his blazer and pulled it tight. Jackson then rubbed his hands rapidly over her arms to provide warmth, and Mary Anne rewarded him with a brief smile. As they walked through the hospital, Mary Anne saw a mother, being pushed in a wheelchair, holding a newborn. She wondered if she had just given birth. It activated a memory of a previous encounter she had while in a similar hospital. She tried her best to avoid hospitals. Jackson took the girls to their appointments, unless it was necessary that she attend. She hoped the patients were getting the proper care, including their daughter Mora. The hospital medicine combined with the unappetizing aroma of their cafeteria food produced a nauseating smell. Dr. Moseley stopped when he reached a rather sizeable room with a rectangular window in the door. Mary Anne looked through the glass and caught a glimpse of Mora sleeping. She was embarrassed because it was her actions that put them in this awful predicament.

"She's sound asleep, but you can wait until she wakes up," Dr. Moseley advised. Mary Anne grabbed Dr. Moseley's hand out of nervousness. Being a father himself, he understood her concern. He held her hand briefly and after a few seconds patted her with his other hand before he released it. He reached over and tapped Jackson on the shoulder.

"As I was looking over the paperwork, I realized I need a couple more pieces of information from you Dr. Manning." Jackson held up his index finger, motioning for Dr. Moseley to give him a moment. He turned toward Mary Anne.

"I'll be back in a few minutes," he replied. He

kissed her on the cheek and headed down the hallway with Dr. Moseley. Mary Anne placed her hand on the doorknob and pushed on the lever until it clicked open. She slowly opened the creaking door. As soon as she could squeeze through the opening, she stepped in the room. She tiptoed in the dark toward the bed and immediately noticed the heavy bandages on her arms and legs. Mary Anne slid the rocking chair from the corner of the room to the left side of Mora's bed. She reached over and caressed Mora's hand. After a few soft strokes, Mora made a few faint moaning noises. Her small fingers gripped the covers. She kicked her legs and wiggled her feet.

"Leave me alone. I don't want to go with you," Mora whispered.

"It's okay, Mora; I'm here." Mary Anne grabbed a few tissues from the table next to Mora's bed and dabbed the sweat that was forming above her daughter's brow. Mora's eyelids lifted. She rubbed her eyes and Mary Anne's face incrementally came into view. Mora looked down at her hands and noticed the bandages. Her heartbeat quickened. Her breaths were fast and shallow. The beads of sweat on her forehead traveled down her mocha cheeks. A shaken Mora sat up and touched her arms and legs.

"What happened? Where am I?" she questioned. Mary Anne placed her right hand against Mora's left cheek and looked deep in her eyes.

"Take slow deep breaths," Mary Anne instructed. Mora followed her mother's suggestion. As she calmed down, her memories returned. After a few deep breaths, she turned her entire body toward the wall away from her mother.

"Why didn't you believe me?" Mora asked. Trickles of tears fell from Mora's eyes and onto her white fluffy pillow. Mary Anne walked to the other side of the bed, wanting to talk to her daughter face to face, but every time she tried, Mora turned her body in the opposite direction.

"Mora, I want to believe you, but...." Mora interrupted her mother.

"This is all your fault, if you would've allowed me one day to be beautiful, then the reflection girl wouldn't have harmed me," Mora scolded.

"You're right and if I could take it back I would," replied Mary Anne.

"Why didn't you come and help me?" Mora asked.

"Mora, when I heard you scream, I came as fast as I could. I attempted to open the door, but it was stuck," Mary Anne pleaded.

"Just leave me alone!" Mora demanded. There was nothing Mary Anne could say to appease her daughter. Mora snatched one of the pillows from off her bed and threw it at her mother. "Get out!" she yelled. A small petite nurse by the name of Betty Harper heard the commotion as she walked by Mora's room. The intense verbal exchange between Mora and her mother prompted her to investigate. She peaked her head inside the room and kindly motioned for Mary Anne to join her in the hallway. Mary Anne hurried toward the nurse curious to see if she had some new information regarding Mora.

"I hate to intrude in family matters, but might I suggest something?" Nurse Harper asked, in the politest tone she could muster. Under different circumstances, Mary Anne would have told the nurse to mind her own business, but because she was so polite and had a warm smile on her face, she decided to hear her out.

"Sure, go ahead," Mary Anne responded.

"Give your daughter a little time to herself. I'm sure she will come around." Mary Anne knew the nurse was right, but there was nothing she hated more than disrespectful children and someone who probably had no kids giving her parenting advice. She swallowed her pride for the sake of Mora's well-being and kindly placed her hand on the nurse's shoulder.

"Thank you; I'll give her some time," responded Mary Anne.

Nurse Harper smiled and squeezed Mary Anne's hand as she made her way into Mora's room. She picked up the pillow and placed Mora's delicate head behind it. She handed her a bottled water along with a few pain pills. Mary Anne watched Mora and the nurse's interaction through the rectangular glass window and wondered how a complete stranger could have a more profound effect on her daughter than she could. She replayed today's fiasco in her mind and contemplated how she would have handled things differently. The muscle tension she experienced in her arms and knots she felt in her stomach showed that her guilt was now manifesting into physical conditions. She regretted how she handled the situation. Her daughter was experiencing severe pain, and it was her fault.

An unshakable shadow of sadness haunted her as she continued to blame herself for her daughter's injuries. A reassuring hand touched her shoulder, and she knew by the firm yet gentle grip who it was. His touched was like a superpower that could alter her disposition at once. She rested her small delicate fingers on his big, hairy masculine hands. He placed his other hand on her shoulder and gave her a mini massage. They both peered into the room at their daughter and wondered how they had gotten themselves into this awful predicament.

"I thought you were finishing the paperwork," Mary Anne replied.

"All finished. How did it go in there?" Jackson asked.

"I upset her," Mary Anne chimed.

"She's upset with us both, but in time this will pass," Jackson grabbed Mary Anne's hand. He intended to lead her into Mora's hospital room, but she did not follow.

"I think it's best that I stay out here. Mora doesn't want me in there," she replied.

"Sure, she does," Jackson added.

"She yelled at me and told me to get out," Mary Anne replied.

"I'll talk to her." Jackson turned and headed into Mora's hospital room but stopped when he felt Mary Anne's gentle touch on his shoulder.

"There's something you should know."

Mary Anne's grave expression gave Jackson cause for concern. She pulled Jackson by the hand away from the door and nervously fidgeted with the buttons on Jackson's blazer that she was still wearing. She pushed a few, wet, strands of her hair behind her ears while her downcast eyes stared at the floor.

"What is it, Mary Anne?" Jackson asked,

concerned. Mary Anne turned to him and blurted out the words as fast as she could.

"Mora let me fall down the steps."

"She what?" Jackson asked. Mary Anne let out a long sigh and talked in a faint whisper.

"After I told her, she could not leave the house dressed inappropriately to meet with some boy, Rain mentioned that I was too hard on her. I took several moments and reflected on the situation and realized that I may have been a little too harsh. So, I went upstairs to apologize and when I reached the top of the steps, Mora was standing there blocking me from reaching the top. I tried to go around her, but she continued to block me. I gripped her arm to move her out of the way, and she snatched her arm from my grasp which caused me to tumble down the steps. That's how I got the cut on my head and this bruise on my leg." Mary Anne lifted up her leg for Jackson to see. Jackson knelled down on one knee and examined it.

"It looks worse than it is. Does it hurt?" he asked.

"Not as much as it did earlier, I can walk without limping," she replied.

"I'll have the nurse get you an ice pack."

"Thank you, Jackson," Mary Anne responded.

"I did not know you were having such severe behavioral problems with Mora," he added.

"We've had some altercations, but nothing of this magnitude." Jackson placed his hand on his head and loosened his tie.

"This is a lot to process," Jackson replied.

"There's more."

"More? I don't know if I can handle more," Mary Anne remained silent and waited for Jackson's approval to continue.

"Go ahead," he instructed. Mary Anne lowered her voice to a whisper and stepped in a little closer toward him.

"Do you remember the hush ghost that Mora claimed haunted her dreams and visited her in her room?" Mary Anne asked.

"I remember. We got up at least one night a week dealing with her and that re-occurring problem," replied Jackson.

"Well, Mora claims that the same hush ghost is now trying to pull her in the mirror," Mary Anne stated.

"A ghost pulling her in a mirror?" Jackson questioned.

"Yes, she's calling it the reflection girl now."

"Mary Anne, our daughter has a mild case of schizophrenia; when she doesn't take her medication, she might hallucinate."

"But she takes her pill every morning, I blend them in her smoothie," Mary Anne countered.

"Even if she takes her medication, there is a possibility she might experience some side effects. Aggression and hallucinations are rare, but they happen," Jackson added.

"But Jackson, have you seen her wounds, that's what's making me wonder if there's some truth to this."

"Some truth about a reflection girl dragging her into a mirror? Mary Anne, Mora is in denial about her condition. Hell, we haven't told Rain because she doesn't want her sister to look at her differently. We may have to consider that she may be harming herself." Mary Anne absorbed the sting of Jackson's words. The thought of her daughter injuring herself was too much to consider. Jackson inched closer toward Mary Anne to comfort her, but she held up her hand and signaled for him to stop.

"I just need a moment to myself," Mary Anne replied. Jackson honored her request. He turned and walked into Mora's hospital room. He wanted to examine her for himself.

12

SPECTACLES

Jackson wished Mary Anne would have brought Mora to a hospital with a better reputation than Valley Memorial. Deep down he understood that she had done her best under the extenuating circumstances. He walked over toward the window and rubbed his finger along the blinds and collected a finger full of dust, as he expected. His mind wondered what other areas were being neglected at this subpar facility. He tried to be grateful for the work the staff was doing to aid in Mora's recovery, but it was hard not to compare every hospital he came in contact with to the state-of-the-art facility that he worked at across town. He couldn't wait until Mora was stable so that he could put her in the hands of a care team that he trusted.

Mora lay motionless on her left side. She wrapped her arms tightly around her pillow as a toddler would their favorite teddy bear. Jackson had a seat in the small and uncomfortable rocking chair by her bed. She knew it was her father by the sweet yet subtle cologne that he wore. She hugged her pillow tighter. Jackson put on his specs and reviewed the notes on her chart. He placed it back at the foot of her bed and lifted Mora's wrist to check her pulse. It was strong and stable. "Mora," Jackson called. She turned toward her father. Her eyes were bloodshot red and swollen from the incessant weeping. Seeing his daughter in this vulnerable state, caused a sudden rush of compassion to wash over him. He held her hand. At first, Mora pulled away, but as he gently stroked her hand, she stopped fighting and allowed him to comfort her. They stared at each other in silence. Jackson's mind drifted to some of his most memorable moments he had shared with his daughter.

He recalled the time he took her to the park to teach her how to ride a bike. She refused his help, determined to figure it out on her own. He reminisced on the times they would get ice cream on Sunday after church. He always had to eat half of it to keep it from melting and dripping onto her Sunday dress. It was at times like these he questioned whether leaving Mary Anne was the right decision. He wondered if his relationships with his daughters would be healthier if he had made a better choice. He scooted his chair toward Mora and leaned in close. "Can I share something with you, that I have only confided to your mother?" Curious, Mora sat up straight, nodded her head and gave him her undivided attention.

"My father, Alan Morris Manning, left us when I was a little boy. I was about twelve when it happened. One day, I ran home from school to show my father I had received an A on my math test, but when I arrived home, I saw police cars parked in front of the house. When I walked in the house, my mother was crying at the kitchen table. The night before, I stayed at my friend's house, so I didn't know that when she woke up that morning my father wasn't by her side. My mother didn't normally worry because my father, a musician, often traveled to provide a living for us. But when she woke up that morning and he wasn't there, she was concerned. Not because he was gone, but because he left without his wallet, clothes, and his favorite suitcase. He always left an itinerary of where he would be, but this time he didn't leave one. He just left without telling us anything. The police told her that she would have to wait a few days before she could file a missing person's report. Then they just left me with my mother as she cried her eyes out at the table.

Every night when he was away playing for some of the biggest jazz musicians, he would call at eight o'clock on the dot. He would sing and play the piano for me. I can still remember sitting on the piano bench with him as he created melodies. Those were some of the best memories of my life. After his abrupt departure, I promised my mom that he would call. I assured her it was a mix up and that he would get in touch with us. That night we both waited by the phone until 8:00 p.m., but there was no call. After about a month of waiting for his phone call, I grew tired of seeing my mother cry, so we stopped waiting.

As the years progressed, my mother began to forget things. At first, it was small things like not locking the door or the television program we watched the night prior. But as time passed, she forgot who my father was and then eventually forgot me. It was at the young age of forty-eight that her doctor diagnosed her with Alzheimer's. I still believe that my father's disappearance caused my mother's illness. I wanted to be a musician like my dad, but after seeing my mother suffer, I studied medicine and the brain. That's why I became a psychiatrist—to help people.

I feel like I have failed you as a father. It was never my intention to vanish from you and Rain's life like my father did mine, but it seems as if I have become the person I hated most. Whenever I offer you medication. It is because I want you to be well. I love you, Mora."

Mora took her thumb and wiped the tear from underneath her father's eye. She knew he meant what he was saying because she had never seen him cry. His absence from their lives was more detrimental than he could have imagined. Jackson thought financial support and frequent visits would be enough. But today, after seeing his daughter hurt and in pain, he realized that nothing in the world was more important to him than his children, and that somehow this was partly his fault. Maybe even all his fault. If he had stayed, Mary Anne would not have to raise them alone. He wondered if they could've salvaged their entangled and complicated relationship.

"Why didn't you share that with us? You told us he died," Mora replied.

"I guess because it was too painful. It still hurts."

"Was the night you studied together the last time you saw him?" Mora questioned.

"Yeah, the crazy thing is, whenever an older man

who resembles him approaches me, I always wonder if he could be my father," replied Jackson.

"I'm sorry that happened to you," Mora stated. Jackson kissed Mora on the forehead.

"Dad, can I share something with you, and can you promise to listen as a father and not as a doctor?" Mora questioned

"I'll do my best," he replied.

Mora paused before uttering her next sentence. She was afraid of how her father would respond to what she was about to divulge. "I know you and mom think I am crazy; but I am not." Jackson was about to speak, but Mora held her hand up to halt his response. She wanted to finish her thought. "The hush ghost that terrorized me as a child is trying to pull me into a mirror and I don't know what to do." Mora burst into tears and buried her face into her father's chest. Jackson patted his daughter on the back as she released all her pent-up emotion. When she was finished, she wiped her nose on her sleeve and waited for her father to respond.

"When is the first time you saw this hush ghost in the mirror?" Jackson asked.

"Today at school in the girl's bathroom," she replied.

Tiny goosebumps formed all over her body as a frosty chill swept through the room. She brought her knees to her chest and wrapped her arms around her legs. Her teeth chattered, and she shook uncontrollably. Mora's peculiar behavior prompted Jackson to place his hands on her shoulders. The coldness of her body alarmed him.

"She's coming. It always gets cold when she comes," Mora stuttered. Jackson turned around and examined the room. The door and the windows were closed.

"Mora, no one is coming. It's probably a side effect from the blood transfusion. Some people have reported having vast changes in body temperature temporarily. I'll ask someone to raise the temperature in your room." Jackson stood up to leave, but Mora grabbed his wrist. The strength of her grip astonished him.

"Mora, Mora," a raspy, child-like voice called. Mora dropped the covers and wrapped herself around her father's arm.

"Did you hear the voice?" Mora stammered.

"What voice?" Jackson asked.

"Sticks and stones rarely break bones, but your evil thoughts will make me harm you," the raspy child-like voice chanted. Mora stepped out of her bed prepared to run as far away from the voice as possible.

Jackson kneeled down until his eyes were

parallel with Mora's. He slid his gold trimmed round spectacles up his narrow nose and placed one of his hands on each side of Mora's face. "Breathe Mora, just breathe." Mora closed her eyes. She took long breaths in and slow breaths out. Her demeanor calmed. When she opened her eyes, she saw a small silhouette figure within the left lens of her father's glasses. She rubbed her eyes and shook her head to ensure her eyes were not playing tricks on her, they weren't. Mora knew exactly who it was when she her hands rise from the side of her body and those oily fingers yellow nails reached toward her. Mora released an ear-piercing scream, smacked the glasses off Jackson's face, and ran toward the door. Jackson fell back grabbed the bottom of Mora's hospital gown before she left the hospital room. He held Mora with one hand while he reached for the panic button on the side of the bed. Seconds later, a rotund woman with light peach-colored skin walked in and saw Mora tussling with her father. She pressed the intercom button.

"I need backup in room 126. I have an unstable patient," she called.

A male nurse entered Mora's room with a long needle in his hand. One nurse held Mora down while the other tried to administer a sedative, but it was a challenge trying to dodge swinging arms and kicking feet. Once they had her restrained, the nurse injected the mild sedative into Mora's arm. After a few minutes passed, Mora's demeanor calmed. Jackson looked at Mora and caressed the left side of her face. *What's wrong with my baby?*

13

AWAKENED

*A*fter a few peaceful hours of rest, an unfamiliar creaking sound jolted Mora from her sleep. She opened her eyes but was afraid to move the thin blanket, that barely covered her feet, from over her head. She silently prayed that the reflection girl wasn't in her room. It was the first time in the last few weeks in which her dreams were not plagued by jarring nightmares, so she remained hopeful. Mora gathered her courage and snatched the blanket from her face and search the room for the source of the creaking sound. The culprit, an empty rocking chair that swayed back and forth in the corner of her room.

An artic chill tarried with in her room. Mora removed the covers from her body. She hopped out of the bed, limped toward the window, and slammed it shut. The only sound she heard now was the beeping hospital monitor by her bed. Mora had a strong urge to urinate but was determined not to use the bathroom until she was in a safer environment. She held her bladder, but her urge to urinate grew more powerful by the minute. Mora crossed her legs in hopes that her urge would dissipate. She felt a warm trickle travel down her thigh, and realized she had no choice but to run to the toilet. She took a book off the small desk and placed it in between the door and the frame to ensure the door stayed open. She flicked on the light switch and closed her eyes as she walked past the bathroom mirror and sat on the toilet. A sense of relief washed over her as she emptied her full bladder. A loud squeaking sound captured her undivided attention. It sounded like a large marker writing against a dry erase board. Mora looked up and saw her name being written in a white and chalky dust color on the mirror.

She jumped up off the toilet and sprinted toward the door. An unseen force pushed the book she placed there several feet away and the door slammed shut. Mora gripped the loosened doorknob with both of her hands and pulled with every ounce of strength she could muster. She was surprised when the doorknob broke, and she fell backwards on the floor. She could hear the volume of her voice decreasing every time she yelled until it evaporated into a whisper and then to nothingness. It was as if someone had a remote control and was decreasing her volume.

Oil-like liquid flowed out of the mirror and spilled onto the sink. Drop by drop, the black tar-like substance built itself into a solid mass that incrementally took on Mora's exact shape. It gripped its claw-like hands at the base of the counter, panted for a few moments and then pounced on the floor. It crawled toward Mora. Every movement of her body sounded as if bones were cracking. Loose strands of her stringy long hair hung in her face. She pounded her hands against the tile floor. The force of her pounds caused Mora to bounce slightly off the ground. Her slightest touch left gaping holes in the ceramic tile. The reflection-girl crawled toward her with her mouth open. Mora searched for something in the bathroom that she could use as a weapon. Behind her was only the toilet. She grabbed the toilet bowl lid and swung it across the reflection girl's face. Mora flew into the bathroom door, and the reflection girl flew across the bathroom in the other direction. Pieces of her ceramic face shattered all over the floor.

"Why do you keep hurting me?" screamed the reflection girl in a demented voice. The broken pieces of her face turned to liquid. They traveled back like small ants being drawn to left open food and within seconds her face was whole again. She turned her head toward Mora. *Click.... click.... click...* was the sound her neck made as her red eyes glowed. She charged toward Mora and slammed her fist into the floor one after the other. Mora crawled back toward the bathroom door as fast as she could, making sure to keep her eyes on the reflection girl. When it reached Mora, she stopped a few inches from her face. Mora could feel her cold, putrid, breath blowing against her body. The reflection girl smiled and revealed her jagged teeth. She caressed Mora's cheek with her bumpy and wet hands. Mora could feel the oily like substance on her skin and trembled in disgust. She stuck out her wet, black, tongue and licked one of Mora's fresh wounds. Then took her thumb and rubbed it over Mora's thick eyebrows. "You pretty; me pretty," The reflection uttered in her demented child-like voice.

Mora pointed at the wall behind her, still unable to speak. The reflection girl turned her head. Mora scooted backward several feet and booted the reflection in the face. They both flew in opposite directions. Mora hit the bathroom door, and heard it click open. She leaped up, open the door, and pushed the desk in her room against it. Mora kept her eyes on the door. Everything stopped. The silence was uncomfortable. She could hear her heart thumping against her rib cage. Mora looked to her left then her right and kept backing away. Her eyes glued on the door. After a few quiet moments of no action she exhaled. She took another step backwards an felt a chilly breeze blow against the back of her neck. When she turned around, the reflection girl was staring her straight in the eyes. A high-pitched squeal escaped her lips, but was muted by the reflection girl's cold, hard, and sticky hands that covered Mora's mouth. The reflection girl dropped to the ground to escape the view of potential bystanders. She clasped her legs around Mora's body which rendered her immobile. She used her right hand to drag Mora and herself along the floor while her left hand was used to muffle Mora's screams. Her extended fingers wrapped themselves around Mora's mouth like sprouting vines. The reflection girl stopped dead in her tracks and sniffed the air. She released Mora, returned into her liquid form, and flowed underneath the crack of the bathroom door. Nurse Betty walked in the room to find Mora on the floor trembling.

"Did... did... you see her?" Mora stuttered, her voice quivering with fear.

"See who?" Nurse Betty asked.

"The reflection girl. She was right here," Mora replied. The nurse had a seat next to Mora on the floor.

"It's okay Mora; there is no girl," she countered.

"She's in the bathroom," Mora replied. Nurse Betty walked in the bathroom, but everything was in order.

"Mora, there is no one in here." Mora did not believe her and limped toward the bathroom to check for herself. To her surprise, there were no holes in the floor, and no broken toilet tops. The desk was positioned back in the corner and the broken knob was now attached to the door.

"She was here! I promise I am not lying," Mora stated.

"Just be calm, Mora. It was probably just a frightful dream."

"It wasn't a freaking dream; she was in my room!" Dr. Moseley, who was outside the door, motioned for Nurse Betty to come toward him.

"I'll be right back," Nurse Betty replied.

"Please don't leave me alone in here!" Mora yelled. Mora held the nurse's arm so tight that Nurse Betty felt her blood flow restrict.

"Let me go," she uttered. She pulled her arms from Mora's grasp then kneeled down in front of Mora.

"I understand you're frightened, but you can see me through the glass," Mora calmed down. Nurse Betty stepped into the hallway and waved at Mora from the window and then turned her undivided attention to Dr. Mosley. Mora darted out of the hospital room like a track star and limped as fast as she could down the hallway.

"Mom! Dad!" Mora yelled.

"Stop her before she hurts herself," Dr. Moseley yelled. An orderly reached for her arm, but Mora swung her fist and hit him with all her might as she continued to limp toward the waiting room. She ran as fast as her injured legs would allow.

A resting Mary Anne sat up in the waiting room and turned toward Jackson. "Did you hear that?" replied Mary Anne.

"Hear what?" Jackson asked.

"I heard Mora's voice," she replied.

"Mora is sleeping Mary Anne; they will let us know when she has awakened," Jackson responded.

"She is not sleeping. I just heard her voice," Mary Anne stood up and ran down the hall searching for Mora. Jackson doubtingly followed her.

"Mora? Mora?" Mary Anne called.

"Mom!" Mary Anne turned down one of the hospital corridors and saw her daughter limping toward her.

"Mom, they don't believe me; she tried to snatch me again," replied Mora.

"It will be okay darling; it's going to be okay." Jackson arrived and stood in between them and the hospital staff. He turned to Mary Anne.

"Head to the car. I'll be there shortly." Dr. Moseley walked close to Jackson and talked in a faint whisper.

"Your daughter is mentally fragile and a danger to herself. It is hospital protocol to keep her here for seventy-two hours," he whispered.

"I'll be damned if I let my daughter stay in this atrocious medical facility for another minute," responded Jackson. Jackson walked out the hospital doors and met up with Mary Anne and Mora. "I'll get the car. Stay with your mother." Mary Anne handed Jackson the keys and put Jackson's sport coat on her shivering daughter. Mary Anne rubbed her hands together and blew hot air on them to keep herself warm. Jackson pulled up with the car and unlocked the doors for them to get in, but Mora did not budge. She stood in her spot as still as a statue.

"What's wrong?" Jackson asked. Mora pointed toward the rearview mirrors.

"She will get me. There are too many mirrors," Mora replied.

"No one's going to get you," Mary Anne responded. Mora ignored her mother, covered her eyes, and refused to get in the car. Jackson opened up the trunk and grabbed the lug wrench and swung it at both side mirrors. When Mora heard the broken glass fall to the ground, she removed her hand from her eyes and examined both mirrors. They were broken. She ran toward her father and hugged him.

He handed Mary Anne the keys and climbed in the back with Mora. Mora looked up and noticed that the rearview mirror was still inside the car. She closed her eyes and pointed. Jackson took the lug wrench in his hand and struck it. It fell off the windshield and onto the dashboard. Mary Anne jumped and shielded her eyes when she heard the loud clash. "Sorry," Jackson replied. Mora laid her head on her father's lap, and he rubbed his hands over the edges of her hair. Mary Anne started the car and slowly backed out of her parking spot. She maneuvered it as safely as possible which proved difficult without mirrors. Jackson's phone rang.

"Hey, Veronica." Mary Anne rolled her eyes. She wished that the rear-view mirror was still attached so that he could see her unpleasant expression.

"Meet me at Mary Anne's house in an hour," Mary Anne paused at the stop sign and turned toward Jackson.

"What am I supposed to do, not answer?" he asked.

"Yes," she replied. Ten minutes later, they

pulled into their subdivision and parked in the driveway. Jackson gave Mora a few lights shoves, and she woke up. He opened the door to lead her into the house.

"I'm not going in the house. This is where she attacked me and attempted to pull me in the mirror," Mora stated.

"I got an idea. Let's tape up every mirror?" Jackson suggested. And if Mary Anne allows it, I'll stay over and sleep in your room. Mora eyed her mother for approval.

"Okay, he can stay," replied Mary Anne. Jackson kissed Mora on the cheek and created a loud smacking sound.

"That is so gross," replied Mora, with a huge grin on her face.

"Stay here and I'll tape the mirrors. No reflection girl will harm my daughter again," Jackson said. He was happy to be present in both their lives. It felt right.

"Do you still keep the tape in the junk drawer?" he asked.

"Yes," replied Mary Anne.

"I will be right back," Mary Anne handed Jackson the keys.

"It's the gold one," said Mary Anne.

"I know. I used to live here, remember?" Mora noticed her mother had a band-aid on her head.

"I'm sorry I made you fall. I didn't want you to get hurt," said Mora.

"When I was seventeen, I got all dolled up for Chad Higgins, the most popular boy in school, but he never came. It was painful and I didn't want that for you."

"I've learned more about you and dad this evening than I have in my whole sixteen years on this Earth. Wouldn't it be easier if you both just shared your experiences with us?" Mora added.

"You're right, I'll do better, but while we're confessing, I might as well tell you chocolate dimples called." Mora fell out on the back seat and put her hands over her face.

"My life is over," Mora replied.

"If you forgive me, I'll bend my make-up rule and might think about giving you a relaxer to straighten your hair." Mora shot up from the back seat with a huge grin on her face.

"Deal!" Mora yelled. Mary Anne reached over and hugged Mora.

"We will get through this," she added. There was a series of knocks on Mary Anne's window.

"It's all done," Jackson said.

"Did you tape the mirror in the hallway?" Mora asked.

"Yes ma'am."

"What about the bedrooms and bathrooms?"

"I covered them all." Mora was relieved. They walked through the entire house and checked to make sure every mirror was covered and then went downstairs. Mora jumped on the couch, grabbed the remote and flipped through the channels on the television. Mary Anne pulled Jackson to the side.

"Did you clean up the blood on the floor in the bathroom?" she asked, in a soft tone.

"I just taped the mirrors. You didn't clean it up?" he questioned.

"No, I was in such a hurry; I drove Mora straight to the hospital."

"It was probably Rain, you know she's a neat freak," he replied.

"If Rain would have saw blood on the floor, she would have called," Mary Anne countered.

"Maybe the hush ghost cleaned it up," Jackson joked.

"That's not funny. Jackson something isn't right," Mary Anne continued.

"You did hit your head and were under a lot of stress. Maybe you cleaned it up and can't remember," he added.

"Maybe you are right," she replied.

"We can discuss this in the morning; you've had a long day." He kissed Mary Anne on the forehead, and she went in the kitchen.

Mary Anne was unsettled. She ran the events of today's fiasco over and over in her mind and she could not remember picking up the blood. She took out a bag of Mora's favorite chips from the pantry and put a frozen pizza in the oven. She left Jackson and Mora sitting on the couch eating potato chips and Halloween candy. She walked up and down the stairs and retraced her steps, but there was not a single drop of blood anywhere. *How could Mora's towel be soaked with blood, but there be no drops of blood anywhere?* Something wasn't right. "I'm going to the bathroom," Mary Anne announced.

Jackson and Mora decided on cartoons after flipping through countless channels. They needed something light-hearted and funny to put a positive spin on the chaotic and challenging day. Mora heard the front doorknob rattle and her eyes darted in that direction. She jumped on the couch and shoved her dad on his right shoulder while she pointed at the front door.

"It's the reflection girl she's back," Mora uttered. The doorknob turned, and the door creaked open. Jackson jumped off the couch and grabbed the bat in the corner. He gripped his hands around the sleek metal handle and held it like a baseball player preparing to slug a home run. He swallowed a huge chunk of air and waited for the unknown intruder to enter their home.

14

INSIDE

Jackson gripped the bat with his sweaty palms, beads of sweat formed on his forehead. The salty residue that traveled down his face and onto his chocolate lips was hard to ignore. His thumping heartbeat multiplied as he watched the gold door handle jiggle from left to right. He lifted the bat a few inches higher. He did his best to hold it steady as his hands trembled and legs shook. Mora ducked behind the back of the sofa and buried her face into the sofa pillow. The door creaked open, and the intruder walked inside. Jackson raised the bat over his head and charged toward the individual. The unknown individual dropped their belongings on the floor, and shielded their hands over their head, fearful of being bludgeoned.

Jackson dropped the bat on the floor, placed one of his hands on the back of the sofa, and waited for his heartbeat to normalize. It was Rain. She stayed on the floor and caught her breath. Jackson walked over to her and offered his hand. After a few seconds and a hostile stare, Rain accepted her

father's hand and stood up.

"You almost killed me!" Rain yelled.

"I'm sorry; we thought you were an intruder," Jackson replied. Mora lifted her head when she heard Rain's voice.

"Intruders don't have keys. Rain swings her house keys in the air and taunts her father. What brings you her? It's not your weekend to have us?" replied Rain.

"Can't a father just come check on my daughters?"

"When Dr. Manning shows up there is always a reason," Rain answered. A familiar and annoying car horn blared outside of their home. "Veronica is outside waiting on you, and she isn't happy." Jackson looked at his phone and realized that he had six missed calls. He grabbed his jacket off the chair and headed out the door but not before placing a wet kiss on Rain and Mora's forehead.

"I'll be right back. Rain, stay in the living room with your sister please?" Jackson exited the front door, careful to lock it behind him. Rain wiped the wet kiss off of her forehead and then slid her hand on her jeans. Rain's eyes shifted toward Mora. Her disposition changed from playful to concerned when she saw Mora bandaged around her wrist and ankles. Rain sat next to her sister, took her hand, and caressed it.

"What happened Mora?" Rain asked, confused. Mora scooted toward her sister.

"I really don't want to talk about it. Every time I tell someone, they don't believe me. Mom and Dad pretend to, but they're just trying to make me feel better," she replied. Rain gazed at her sister dead in her eyes and wiped the tears that flowed down her cheeks.

"Mora. You can tell me anything," she stated. Mora took a deep breath before going into her story. "Do you remember the reflection ghost that used to frighten me as a child?"

"How could anyone forget. Your screams woke up the entire house," Rain replied.

Mora leaned in close to Rain. "I see her when I look in the mirror. She's been trying to pull me through it," Mora whispered.

"Come again?" asked Rain.

"You heard me correctly. She did this to me," Mora lifted her arms and unwrapped the bandages.

"Mora, I think you should keep the bandages wrapped; they put them on for a reason," Rain suggested.

"Rain, you need to see this," Mora replied. Mora continued to unwrap the bandages, but when she showed her arms to her sister. Her skin was perfect and whole. Mora stared at her arms in disbelief unable to comprehend why she had no wounds. "I don't understand. I had lacerations and cuts on my arms and legs. That's why Dad is here. I had a blood transfusion and everything." Mora removed the bandages from her legs and ankles to inspect her wounds, but they were perfect and whole.

"Mora it's okay; I believe you." Rain replied.

"I think I'm going crazy," Mora replied.

"Quit saying things like that. Hurry up and rewrap your legs and arms and don't mention this to anyone," Rain replied.

"Shouldn't I tell Mom and Dad?" Mora asked.

"Dad's a psychiatrist; he will probably medicate you," Rain replied. Mora broke her gaze from Rain and stared at the floor.

"Have they already medicated you?" Rain asked, curiously.

"Since I was eight," Mora replied. Rain playfully hit Mora upside the head.

"Ouch, that hurt," Mora whined.

"You deserved it; you know we don't keep secrets. Why didn't you tell me?" Rain replied.

"I didn't need you thinking I was crazy too," Mora replied.

"Everybody has a lil crazy in them. Trust me you are not alone," she replied.

Mora chuckled. "Thanks, for believing me," Mora replied.

"You'd do the same for me. Let's discuss this in more detail when Mom and Dad aren't around."

Jackson walked out on the front porch and fired up a cigarette. It was a stressful day and although he had quit smoking years ago, he needed to feel that smooth menthol flow through his lungs. It was one of the few things that provided him a feeling of peace. Veronica stepped out of her black Range Rover and leaned against the car with her arms crossed. She had a beautifully wrapped gift in her hand. Jackson walked toward Veronica and stood next to her. She placed the gift in his hand and resumed her original stance.

"Where is your yellow medallion," Jackson asked.

"You noticed?" Veronica questioned.

"When you've been with someone off and on for 18 years, you notice when they aren't wearing something, they've worn every day."

"I've decided to give it to Mora as a birthday gift. It's in three days."

"I don't forget birthday's Veronica. I had her gift hand crafted," Jackson replied.

"What did you get her?" Veronica asked?

"It's a secret. I'm sure she will call you once she gets your gift. You can ask her then," Jackson replied. There is a long awkward pause between them. Veronica turned toward Jackson.

"You should have told me Mora was seeing things," Veronica stated.

"How did you find out?" Jackson asked.

"I can be very persuasive Jackson, you of all people should know," she added. She reached her hand through the car window and grabbed a folder from the passenger seat. It was Mora's hospital records from today's encounter. "Things like this need to be destroyed. It's damaging for your career and for *our* Mora. Could you imagine if someone from her school found out about this? The last thing we need is for Child Protective Services to take our daughter away from us. Jackson took the file, folded it, and placed it inside the back of his pants.

"How long has this been happening?" she asked.

"She's not your daughter Veronica. Mary Anne and I are handling it," Jackson replied.

"She's as much my daughter as she is Mary Anne's," Veronica countered.

"No, you were the surrogate. Mary Anne is the birth mother, we have documentation to confirm this, remember?" Jackson reminded.

"Is that all I am to you? A surrogate?" she asked.

"That's not what I said," Jackson responded.

"So, what are you saying Jackson?" Veronica asked.

"I'm saying, I think we should take some time apart," Jackson replied.

"So, you're abandoning me while I'm pregnant with your child?" she asked. Jackson took a more serious tone. He lowered his voice and turned to face Veronica.

"I'll be there for my child, but Mora and Rain need me now. They need their father," Jackson replied.

"You still love her."

"She's the mother of my children, I will always love Mary Anne."

"No, you're still in love with her. What kind of man chooses their ex over their fiancée?"

"Veronica, my daughter needs me. Mora tried to harm herself," Jackson responded. Veronica ran toward the house to check on Mora, but Jackson grabbed her hand and pulled her back toward him.

"I need to talk to her, to make sure she's okay!" Veronica countered.

"This isn't the time."

"It's never the right time," she added. She snatched her arm away from him and pointed her finger in his face.

"Twenty-four-hours and the boil comes to a head!" Veronica yelled. She slammed her fist on the hood of the Range Rover, jumped inside, and zoomed down the street. Jackson had never seen her that angry, then again, he had never told her no. This wasn't an empty threat. He had to get in front of the situation. He took a few deep puffs of his cigarette, stomped out the light, and headed back in the house with Mora's gift in hand.

When he walked through the door. Mora noticed the large, gift-wrapped boxes in his hand. Her eyes widened with excitement. "Did you buy me a gift?" she asked.

"After you scolded me about handing you cash, I got something more heartfelt. I hope you like it. Happy early birthday." Jackson responded.

Mora snatched the package from Jackson. She shook it, excited about its contents. She removed the pretty bow. She always appreciated delicately wrapped gifts because she liked to preserve the packaging. Mary Anne was in the kitchen placing slices of pizza on paper plates while Jackson, and Rain watched as Mora opened up her present. It was like a mini Christmas with the complete family there. It was comforting to see Mora smile. Mora opened the packaging being sure to keep the colorful tissue paper intact. Inside the big box were two boxes, a small gold and crimson box and a black box. She opened the gold and crimson box first. Inside it was a yellow diamond amulet necklace. On the front of the gold encased amulet was her name, *Mora,* and on the back in faded lettering it said *Karma.* There was a note inside. It read:

To Mora,

This has been in my family for years. My parents gave it to me and now I am passing it on to you. I hope it brings you as much good as it has brought me. May it protect and guide you as it has me.

Happy Birthday,

Veronica.

"Wow, Veronica gave me her necklace. It's beautiful." Mora replied. Mary Anne went into the freezer, took out the ice tray, and slammed it on the counter. Jackson stared in her direction and she cut him an evil stare.

"Let me put it on you," Rain suggested. Mora handed Rain the necklace. She turned around and allowed Rain to clasp it around her neck. "It's beautiful Mora," Rain replied.

"Veronica always has the prettiest things. Let's invite her over so I can tell her thank you," Mora suggested.

"It's kind of late. Let's talk to her in the morning. Why don't you open up my gift," Jackson suggested? Mora opened the black box. Inside was a purple jewelry box that had the words *Mora's Jewelry Box* in black lettering across the top.

"I was saving it to give to you on your birthday, but I thought now was the perfect time. The song it plays is the song my father used to play on the piano for me. Open it," Jackson encouraged. An excited Mora held it up for Mary Anne to see.

"It's a jewelry box. I've always wanted one of these," Mora replied. When Mary Anne saw the jewelry box, she came from behind the kitchen table and walked toward Mora.

"Mora don't open it!" she yelled.

"Mary Anne, it's just a jewelry box," interrupted Jackson. Mary Anne walked faster toward Mora.

"Give me the jewelry box, Mora!" Mary Anne demanded.

"Why are you trying to take this from me?" Mora asked as she held it close to her chest.

"Mom, it's not that serious," Rain demanded.

Jackson grabbed Mary Anne to keep her from taking Mora's gift. Mary Anne snatched her arm from his grip and jumped toward Mora and grabbed the bottom of the jewelry box. Mora held on to the top while Mary Anne tightened her grip on the bottom half. They tussled with it until it broke. Mary Anne flew across the room with the bottom half, while Mora held the top half.

"You broke it!" I don't forgive you! I hate you and wish you were not my mother!" she yelled.

Mora looked down at the top half of the jewelry box and screamed. Inside the top of the jewelry box was a mirror and within it was the reflection girl. Mora tried to let go of the box, but her hands were glued to it. The reflection's liquid-like hands jolted out of the mirror and wrapped themselves around Mora's body. Her crystal-like yellow nails dug deep into her skin, and drops of her precious blood dripped to the floor along with Mora's purple glasses.

"If you can't love me on the outside, maybe you can love me from within," the reflection's voice bellowed. Mora's body became like-fluid and the reflection girl snatched her into the mirror. The top of the jewelry box fell to the ground, and the mirror broke into a plethora of pieces. Mary Anne screamed, Rain fainted, and Jackson stood there paralyzed with fear as Mora's cell phone vibrated on the kitchen counter.

Want to know what happened to Mora? Continue the story by purchasing the next book in the series Mora's Acceptance on Amazon.

GET EXCLUSIVE MATERIAL FROM C.F. EDWARDS

If you want to find out what happened to Mora, join my VIP reader group for information on upcoming books and to get your free starter C.F. Edwards library:

1. A free copy of Volonians: Mysteries of the Vondercrat.
2. A sneak peak of Mora's Acceptance .

Get your free content by signing up at my website: www.cfedwards.com

LEAVE A REVIEW!

Dear Readers,

Thank you for taking time out to read my story. There is no feeling that compares to creating a story and having someone read the words you have written. I am forever grateful for you taking the time out to read my book.

Reviews help independent authors gain more visibility and provide us with an opportunity to build a career as a writer. If you enjoyed the story, feel free to leave an honest review. I love hearing what my readers think about the words I have created, and I am sure future readers will as well.

Please leave a review on amazon.

ABOUT THE AUTHOR
UNSTEREOTYPICAL DEFINITION

Unstereotypical - *Not adhering to a widely held, oversimplified viewpoint of a person, place, thing, or idea.*

The Unstereotypical book series is a collection of weird stories. The people, places, things, or ideas do not fit the mold of what is usually expected. These stories are uncanny and do not ascribe to the oversimplified stereotypical rules most stories are accustomed to following. For example, the stories have a variety of lengths that range from short story to novel length. It is always best to start with Book #1 of each series/serial so you can have a smooth, uninterrupted reading experience. Each book picks up exactly where the last one left off. Think Netflix for books. I have an Unstereotypical brain, and this is how I tell stories. I am a lover of books, television, and movies, and those mediums have influenced my writing and the way I create.

Another way these books differ from others is they **rarely** reveal the ethnicities/races of the characters in these stories. I describe their skin tones with adjectives such as vanilla, peach, mocha, chocolate, cinnamon, bronze, and a range of other flavors and colors. I purposely did this, because while growing up there were few books, TV shows, and films in the genres I enjoyed where I felt represented. It's my desire for people of **all** backgrounds to experience and see themselves in these stories, so I made the races of these characters ambiguous. The reader gets to imagine the character how they envision them in their mind.

These books are for anyone who has ever felt like they do not fit in with the masses. They are for people who have felt misunderstood, weird, or as if they don't belong, because I know what that feels like. Each story is told to make us feel empathetic toward one another as humans. Everyone has something they are struggling with. If you have ever felt different, weird, or not normal, then these books are for you.

I wrote these books for Unstereotypical Readers. If you are reading this, just know I created this book for you. I hope you enjoy these stories, and I appreciate you for taking the time to purchase and read the eccentric thoughts, words, and dreams from this Unstereotypical Author.

I am the co-author of the Volonian Series, and

sole author of the Unstereotypicals Series and many more to come. I enjoy coffee, ice-cream and posting uplifting quotes via social media. Feel free to send me an email. I'll reply back.

For more information:
www.cfedwards.com
chris@cfedwards.com

facebook.com/cfedwardsjr
twitter.com/cfedwards_
instagram.com/cfedwards_

BOOKS BY C. F. EDWARDS

In the Unstereotypicals Series

Mora

A young girl sees a horrifying reflection of herself and has to learn to love herself or risk living a real-life nightmare.

Gift Mora to a friend.

Mora's Acceptance

After an intense battle with her reflection Mora awakens in an unfamiliar place with unfamiliar people and unanswered questions.

Purchase Mora's Acceptance on amazon.

In the Volonian Series

A class six witch, by the name of Varah Cutter has conjured the Vondercrat, a forbidden book of spells that controls the magic of all the Volonian people and has no idea how she has done it. Varah and her two young children, Broc and Shenzara run from the five Lords who oversee the planet in hopes of escaping their sentencing but run into heaps of trouble along the way.

Download Mysteries of the Vondercrat for free.

Awakening of The Au Vyndure

Broc and Shenzara are separated from their mother and are all alone. They have 72 hours to accept the power bestowed to them or risk their whole planet being destroyed and placed in the hands of a demented evil who wants nothing more than to control the planets power and the inhabitants within.

Purchase Awakening of The Au Vyndure on amazon.

ACKNOWLEDGMENTS

During my teenage years, I use to have really weird, crazy, and bizarre dreams. Once I awakened, I would run upstairs and tell my mother all about them. She always patiently listened and when I was finished, she told me. "Boy, write those crazy ideas down and put them in a book because they could be movies, television shows, and make us rich." Well mom, I wrote them down and put a few of those ideas in this book. They haven't been adapted to film and television or made us rich yet, but I feel rich and blessed to have such an understanding, caring, and supportive mother. If only Mora had parents like you...

When I doubted if I could write my own book, you always told me that I could do it. If it were not for you planting those seeds in my subconscious as a child and continuing to water them, this book would not exist. I love you.

Made in the USA
Middletown, DE
21 September 2022